My Family and other freaks

My Family and other freaks

Carol Midgley

Quercus

First published in Great Britain in 2012 by

Quercus
55 Baker Street
7th Floor, South Block
London
W1U 8EW

A CIP catalogue record for this book is available from the British Library

ISBN 978 0 85738 894 0

1 3 5 7 9 10 8 6 4 2

For lovely Lucy, who makes me

laugh every day

I am writing this diary beneath my new Ikea duvet cover. I'm sweating like a pig on a sunlounger. A mousey-haired pig with blackheads if you want the full 3D picture. I may die from suffocation, but this is probably for the best. My life is so O.V.E.R. I cannot set foot in school ever again. I would die of shame. So, whichever way you look at it, I'm dead.

Am never coming out, even though *Britain's Got Talent* is on.

7.10 p.m.

Hmmm. *Britain's Got Talent* sounds quite good. Dad is downstairs winding up my little sister Phoebe. It's his usual trick of picking up the phone and pretending to book himself on the programme. 'I'm going to fart the National Anthem on stage,' he says down the phone, all serious as though he's talking to the producer.

Phoebe, who has just turned three and believes literally everything she's told, is trying to grab it off him crying, 'No, Daddy, pleeeeese don't trump on telly.'

This is quite funny, but I must not be tempted. I hate my parents. Hate them. If they hadn't been canoodling on the sofa again (snogging at their age – in front of me! It's practically child abuse) I wouldn't have had to take the dog for a walk to avoid puking up and then I wouldn't have bumped into HIM – Damian Griffiths from our year – dreamy, delicious, divine Damian as Megan calls him (she reckons she's good at English but she just looks in a Roger's Thesawhateveritis) and suffered the biggest humiliation of my 12 sorry years of life.

Why are my mum and dad like this? Why can't they be like normal parents and get a divorce? My friends don't know how lucky they are having parents who hate each other. Stupidly in-love parents are a curse. My dad – and this is totally gross – pinches my mum's bum and his face goes all pink and he says, 'Ooh you've still got the body of an 18-year-old.'

Hello? Is the man blind? How many 18-year-olds do you see with bingo wings and a caesarean scar? Emily Morgan's big sister is 18 and she's got a figure like Beyoncé. Mick Taylforth (who's a bit of a perv) says she's 'fit as a butcher's dog' and you could 'bounce a tennis ball off her bum'. I think that's a compliment. Whereas my mum is forty-bloody-four with a backside like a blancmange. So my dad's a liar as well as a bad father.

My brother, Rick, who's 15 and growing his hair long and mostly ignores me because I am a 'loser' (this from a boy whose room, the Stink Pit, smells like a wrestler's bottom – not that I've ever gone up to a wrestler and smelled his bottom), well, he says they're both selfish, and if we have any hope of going to university they'll have to split up or at the very least lose their jobs because universities only want kids from underprivileged backgrounds now. Fiona Wilde's dad left her mum for a barmaid and took her to Lanzarote and now Fiona's form teacher, Mrs Ryan, is dead nice to her and says, 'It's OK if you're late with your homework, Fiona. I know your life is chaotic at the moment.' Chaotic? She wants to come round to our house/hovel some time. Rick says Fiona could get to any uni she wanted now without doing any work because she's officially from a 'dysfunctional home'.

Dysfunctional? University people are supposed to be clever, but they clearly don't know the meaning of the word. Am too upset to write any more now. If this diary suddenly stops, it means I have died from ~~asfixya~~ ~~asphixiasion~~ not enough air.

7.13 p.m.

Should somebody one day find my corpse and need to know why I lie here, this is my official last testament.

What happened was this: I took Simon to the park (that's the dog – he's named after Simon Cowell because his teeth are really white) but first went to the cupboard under the kitchen sink to get poop-scoop bags. Except of course there were none left because my mum's too busy flirting with Dad to ever bother doing the shopping so I had to take a Tesco carrier bag instead. Simon was very well behaved – by his standards, anyway. He only burst one toddler's ball, though he did cock his leg up on someone's picnic basket but I don't think they noticed. Anyway, he did his poo; it makes me laugh because he always dances round in these tight circles before he 'stoops to poop'. I picked it up because I'm a responsible citizen. It was DISGUSTING and all runny because Phoebe secretly fed him her porridge this morning when Mum wasn't looking. I tied a knot in the top of the bag and was looking for a bin when I saw him. Damian. This is the boy I have spent most biology, maths and English lessons staring at for the past six months. He is The One.

He was sitting down chewing a piece of grass in a really cool way with Sean O'Connor, who's a bit too weird and shy for my liking, but apparently can play the guitar so qualifies as acceptable even though he's got nerdy hair.

'Hi,' I said all casual and sophisticated – well, as sophisticated as you can be while swinging half a kilo of dog diarrhoea. I call Simon to heel because I want to look like a woman in control.

'Cool dog,' says Damian.

'Thanks,' I say, trying to pull back my jacket so they can see the T-shirt Amber bought me which shows I am sponsoring an endangered cheetah. 'We got him from a rescue shelter. He'd been tied to a railing outside Asda and left there. It took nine hours for the man who collects the trolleys to realize he'd been abandoned. He was so thin they couldn't even tell what breed he was.'

'What breed is he?' they both ask at the same time.

'A Labrador/Alsatian/spaniel/beagle cross,' I say proudly. It's very rare.

'They should bring back the firing squad for people like that,' said Sean, which to be honest was the most I've ever heard him speak. Then he said he was getting a collie from a rescue centre as soon as his dad had cleared the rusty bikes out of the backyard.

This was GREAT – me basking as a rescuing heroine, them both stroking Simon, who was wiggling his bottom really sweetly and only trying to hump their legs a little bit, when suddenly Damian leaped back screaming, 'Ugggh! Get it away from me. Get it OFF!!'

At first I thought he meant Simon and was thinking, Well, make your mind up, matey. You were all over him five seconds ago – but then I saw what he was pointing at: the carrier bag from hell. Yellowy poo was spraying out of the bottom. It was spattered all over Damian's jeans like mustard, and they were his best ones from Topman, apparently. Oh Lord and Father, I'd forgotten that supermarkets now put air holes in carrier bags so stupid toddlers don't put them on their heads and suffocate. Thanks, darling Mother. Not only am I now humiliated in front of the most gorgeous boy in school, whom I'd planned to marry but who now hates me, you apparently don't care if I die of toxomplaswhateveritis. I could end up blind or dead or, worse, having to wear bifocal glasses. Never mind Fiona Wilde – it's me who should be seeing a child therapist.

8 p.m.

Am definitely reporting my parents to the police for child cruelty. Just been downstairs for a Mini Milk from the freezer and foolishly told them what had happened and how I wanted to die or at least change schools. They were all weird and silent at first. Then I noticed Dad's shoulders were shaking and Mum was holding her *Take a Break* magazine up to her face. They were LAUGHING.

'I'm glad you think your daughter being ostracized and sinking into childhood depression is funny,' I screech.

'You're not ostrich-sized!' says Phoebe. 'You're much bigger!'

Why is this child not in bed by now?

'Oh, I wish someone had had a camera,' is all Dad said. It's the first time I've ever heard him say anything positive about Simon. Normally he just makes sick jokes about the time he went to South Korea and ate dog (note to self – am never going to that sick country). He thinks it amusing to shout 'boshintang' in Simon's ear. Boshintang is dog-meat soup, but my dad is stupid because Simon can't even speak Korean. Dad says we're too soppy about animals in this country, and that something has gone wrong with evolution when it's humans walking behind dogs carrying their sh** in a bag.

Sore point, actually.

But then when he's on his own in the kitchen

with Simon I hear him talking to him in a baby voice. 'Do you want a Bonio, little lad?' – that sort of thing. So he's a fraud as well as a liar and a bad father.

10 p.m.

Text Amber with an SOS. 'Def leavin home at 16,' I write. 'Major crisis. BTW can I copy yr French homework? xx'. Well, I hardly have time to think about some stupid essay called 'Les Vacances' (très original, professeurs) with MY problems.

Amber is my best friend. I've known her since we were two; we used to live on the same street and, as our mothers never tire of telling us, we were potty-trained together. Some people don't get Amber because she's a bit quiet and serious and obsessed with the environment. Sometimes – and I'm only saying this because I care – she can look spotty because she won't wear make-up to cover them and only uses this non-toxic soap which is made from grass or elephant poo or something. But she's very funny and loyal and always there for me in a crisis.

Except now. Why hasn't she replied to my text? Silly cow's probably forgotten to charge her phone. Why can't people be more organized? What if her best friend needed her? Must I be forever surrounded by selfish people? These are the questions of my so-called life.

Monday

5.30 a.m.

Had a terrible dream that Damian's mother was chasing me down the street with the dog-dirt jeans. I tried to run away but something was weighing my legs down. Wake up to find that it is Simon asleep, lying across my calves. I shove him off and he wriggles up the bed on his belly to lick my face. He knows I am hurting inside and he's trying to comfort me. We have telepathy. I fall back to sleep with four stone of mongrel snoring in my ear and his paw on my shoulder. Bless his little rescue-dog heart – this is his way of thanking me for saving him from death row.

7.30 a.m.

Evil mother says I can't miss school because then she'll go to prison like that woman in the papers from Devon whose daughter had 94 days off. I say, 'Mother, you should go to jail anyway for neglect.'

Phoebe says, 'What's necklect?'

'When your parents don't look after you properly,' I tell her.

'Oooh, I'm necklected!' she says. 'There's no cheese strings left.'

'Exactly,' I say.

I go upstairs to feed Deirdre, my degu, whose stinky cage is now on the shelf in my bedroom because Simon keeps pushing his nose through the bars and nearly giving her a heart attack. Everyone thinks she's an overweight gerbil, but they are ignoramuses. She is actually part of the chinchilla family and a very exotic rodent, although in her home country of Chile they call degus brush-tailed rats. She's the only one in the house who doesn't try to ruin my life.

7.45 a.m.

Correction. Deirdre is also trying to ruin my life. She bit my finger, little stinking rat, and I was only trying to remove a bit of apple that had gone brown to stop her getting ill. Stupid, ungrateful, smelly, fat gerbil. I might put her in her exercise ball later and let the dog push her round the room with his nose to teach her a lesson. It's cruel but, let's face it, funny. Last time Phoebe clapped her hands and said, 'Deirdre disco ball! Again. Again!'

Can the RSPCA point cameras through people's windows?

8.00 a.m.

My finger's dripping blood and it's art today. I need a plaster but, quelle surprise, we've run out. My mother is a slattern (we learned this word in English. It means 'a slovenly woman'), so I have to wrap toilet paper round it and it's all tatty like a First World War wound. My mum doesn't seem to care because she's listening to Chris Evans on Radio 2 and laughing at some kid who's rung in to say his spaniel ate his homework and is now pooing an essay on Macbeth. I don't mean to be rude, but if I had a live spot on national radio I'd say something a bit more amusing than THAT.

8.25 a.m.

Amber is at the bus stop. 'Didn't you get my text?' I say huffily.

'Yes, didn't you get mine?' she says.

I look at my phone. I've forgotten to charge it and the battery's dead. Bah. I tell Amber in full about the poo incident. She is snuffling and snorting with laughter. 'Shut UP!' I say, a bit tearily, so she puts her arm on my back which is the signal that she's sorry. 'This is the boy I love-lust,' I wail. 'What if he never speaks to me again? It will be like someone has switched the light off in my life. Everything will be in black and white, not colour.'

'Oh, for God's sake,' says Amber, 'don't be such a drama queen.' She can be very snappish.

'If he never speaks to you again over that then he wasn't worth it in the first place. Besides, he and his mates are so worried about looking cool he probably hasn't told anyone.'

This might be true. Amber wants to help the planet when she grows up and, like all do-gooders, naively sees the positive side of everything, but please let her be right this time. Amber doesn't really get what I see in the gorgeous Damian, but then this is a girl who is genuinely interested in algae, so she's hardly normal, is she?

8.30 a.m.

Darling brother Rick arrives at the bus stop with two of his too-cool-for-school mates and totally ignores me. Why are they all growing their hair? Why do they call each other 'bro'? Do they think they're living in the Bronx?

'Hello, big bro,' I say, just to annoy him.

'Get lost,' he says, and gives me one of his

withering looks. He thinks the dog-poo incident is another example of my cretinousness and says from now on he's going to pretend that I never existed.

'This is why I'm sometimes glad I don't have a sibling,' says Amber, handing me the French homework. Amber is so right about everything.

9.05 a.m.

Amber is so wrong about everything. Written in huge letters on the form-room whiteboard are the words 'Dench the Stench' with wavy 'smell' marks coming off them. Everyone knows. Everyone is laughing. Even Fiona Wilde is sniggering, and her miserable gob virtually never cracks a smile. This is mental cruelty. Why am I not being offered counselling? Thank God Damian's not in my form or I'd jump out of the window. Amber helps me rub it off the board, but I can see she's smirking. To make myself feel better I tell her, 'That spot on your cheek is oozing pus.' She runs off to the toilets clutching her cheek. Well, if your best mate won't tell you these things, who will?

10.30 a.m.

I hate biology. Hate, hate, hate it. Who gives a stuff how plants reproduce? Or that worms clean up the soil? I'm never going to chuffing eat soil, am I? Amber says it's the key to life. Key to dying of boredom more like. Hopefully Miss Judd, the teacher, is ill again. She's always ill, or late. Megan reckons she's having an affair with Mr McKay, the PE teacher. Ugh, he has nose hair and always smells of coffee. No wonder she's ill all the time.

Damian's in this class; he's ignoring me. He walks past quickly as if he thinks I've got another loaded poop-scoop bag hidden in my satchel which I'm going to pour over his head. He looks really handsome with his dark hair curling over his white collar. I get butterflies when I look at him. Well, more like big flapping moths actually.

Maybe I should just go over and try to make a joke of it all. I will, I will. We're all grown-ups here, aren't we?

10.32 a.m.

Oh, dear God, no. Treasure 'check me out, boys' Cavendish is walking towards him. What kind of person calls themselves Treasure, eh? Her mum and dad chose it when she was born because she was their 'little treasure.' But since this fact would make you vomit every single day of your life, you'd just change it by deed poll as soon as you were old enough to hold a pen, wouldn't you? But she hasn't. She actually LIKES it – and that's all you need to know about Treasure Cavendish. She knows I fancy Damian because Emily Morgan told her. Little snitch. I must remember to accidentally tell Andrew Slater, who she's got a big crush on, that she still gets in bed with her mum and dad.

Treasure's got mascara on again, which is against the school rules, actually. Her eyelashes look like tarantulas' legs, all curled upwards (must get Mum to buy me some of that). Her skin is even more orange than usual, like one of the Mr Men. Little Miss Vain. Hahaha. Her mum's obviously taken her to the beauty salon for another St Tropez spray job (must persuade Mum to take me for one of them). She is gorgeous. No point denying it. Even Amber admits she's pretty, although she says, 'Real beauty is not how you look but purity of thought and deed.' Honestly, I worry about that girl.

Treasure is leaning over so her long hair (bleached, I might add) tumbles down on Damian's desk like something from a bleeding shampoo advert and she's showing him something on her phone. He's smiling. He looks amazing when he smiles. Now I've got washing-machine stomach again. Actually, hello? We're not even allowed to have our phones on in school; I'm telling Miss Judd when she arrives. Why doesn't the woman hurry up?

Treasure must notice me scowling at her because as she walks back to her desk she stage-whispers to me, 'I hope you've washed your hands, Dench. Or don't you bother with soap on Planet Clampett?'

Pause while I contain my rage. Treasure always calls my family the Clampetts, which she seems to think is really clever because it's what her mum (big snob) always calls scruffy people. Apparently it's from some programme called the *Beverly Hillbillies,* which people used to watch about 100 years ago. Just because there are very tall weeds in our garden and our car bonnet's a different colour to the rest of the car.

A few people sitting nearby heard what she said and are laughing. I want to cry but I decide to return fire instead. 'I'd have thought you're more in need of soap than me, Treasure. You know, to wash off all that fake tan. What shade is it today – Tango or Irn-Bru?'

Hooray – everyone's laughing with me not at me now. Oh, apart from Damian, who's glaring. Why did he have to be the only one who didn't find that funny? He fancies Treasure. It's so obvious. I can see weird Sean O'Connor putting his hand over his face so Damian can't see he's sniggering at my rapier wit. Why can't Damian realize how amusing/interesting/quite-good-looking-apart-from-my-nose I am?

10.33 a.m.

Great. Miss Judd was standing behind me and heard what I said. I have to stay behind after class. Treasure is smiling triumphantly. I can practically see my reflection in her whitened teeth.

'Is there a problem between you and Treasure?' she asks at the end of the lesson. 'No, miss,' I lie.

'Because I will not tolerate bullying in my

class,' she says. She has Biro marks on her jumper. Very sloppy. I know from experience that Biro doesn't come out.

'Bullying?' I say. 'Don't make me laugh. Lord Voldemort would have his work cut out bullying her.'

'Don't get lippy with me,' says Miss Judd. 'You're in detention on Thursday.'

Oh no. I said I'd go and see Phoebe doing a little show in her ballet class at 4.30 p.m. on Thursday. She'll hate me now too. Everything is against me. So no change there.

5 p.m.

Rick is in the kitchen teaching Simon to shake hands and roll over. He thumps his tail on the floor when he sees me (Simon not Rick) and wiggles his bum.

'Did you see dream-boy?' says my darling brother, sarcastically but at least not greeting me with a sentence that begins with 'go away'.

'If you mean Damian, he's been fine about it – really cool actually,' I lie. 'Anyway – why do you care?'

Turns out Rick knows Damian's brother Liam in Year 11. Rick says that Liam says Damian's mum washed the jeans and luckily thought it was hilarious. He also said Damian was a 'little pain in the butt' who is always nicking his designer hair wax. I inform him that my Damian does NOT use designer hair wax, although the truth is I did once notice a big clump of it at the back of his head and spent all day wanting to brush it off for him.

'Anyway,' I say, wanting to change the subject, 'Simon's MY dog. I should be the one to teach him tricks.'

'Great,' says evil Dad, arriving home from work. 'Can one of you teach him to go and play on the railway lines?'

I tell evil Mum that because she made me go to school I am now a) a laughing stock, and b) in detention.

She's not even listening and just stares out the window saying, 'Well, it's not the end of the world, love. Just wait until you've got real problems to cope with.' Oh please. As if adults ever have real problems. They don't even have to do homework or exams or face the boy of their dreams every day, who think's they are Sewer Girl. All adults care about is turning the central heating off and eating broccoli. What I'd give to only have that to worry about. Anyway, she's not the one doing detention with Mr Biggins, or, to give him his full name, Biggins Bad Breath Causes Instant Death.

Thursday

12.30 p.m.

Bump into Damian in the dining hall and drop my banana on his foot. He picks it up and hands it back. 'Thanks!' I say.

'No worries,' he says.

'Really sorry about the other day,' I say, shaking a little.

'Just forget it,' he says a bit snappily, walking away with Andrew Slater, one of his cool cronies, who's staring over at me like I'm a freakish bearded lady or something. They go and sit at the table the very furthest away from mine. I think he's overreacting a BIT. I mean, I did apologize and offer at the time to get the trousers cleaned, but Damian just said, 'Yeah, right. I'll just strip off in the park then and walk home in my undies, shall I?'

Still he did just say, 'Forget it,' didn't he? AND he gave me back my banana. This is progress. Andrew Slater can boil his head. Anyway, I've noticed from here that he's got a fat neck.

4 p.m.

Oh God. I'm doing detention with Mick Taylforth, the school perv/psycho. 'Ha, it's Dench the Stench,' he says. So original, Mickey the Thicky.

There's lots of things I could say here about him being really dumb and his dad being in jail for selling stolen mobile phones in the pub (my brother says), but he's too scary. So I just say, 'You've got tomato ketchup all down your jumper.'

Bad-breath Biggins makes us check under all the desks and chairs for chewing gum, clean the brushes in the art room and then read a pamphlet on bullying.

'Bullying ruins lives. Bullies are cowards,' it says. I tell Mr Biggins that for the last time I WAS NOT BULLYING Treasure Cavendish. It was her being nasty to me and my family.

'Well, you two don't spoil a pair,' he says. How dare he? What does he mean? I'm the opposite to Treasure in every single possible way.

5 p.m.

Phoebe looks so sweet in her ballet dress. But she's not speaking to me because I didn't see her do her Teddy Bear's Picnic bit on stage. 'You can't come to my birthday party now,' she says, folding her chubby arms. I don't have the heart to tell her that her birthday's nine months away. But then she notices that I've bought her a Flump and so I am forgiven.

7 p.m.

Mum comes into my bedroom to ask if I'm OK. Behind her back is a bag. She has bought me a new sparkly top from Tesco. When will my mother learn that I disagree with supermarket clothes? Amber says it's all made by child workers getting paid 5p a year or something. It is unethical. Mind you, it's quite a nice top and will go with my white jeans. I decide that I will accept it since my mother needs encouraging to go to the supermarket more often.

Simon's being really cute, guarding Mum's Ugg boots and snuggling up to them. He thinks they're his girlfriend and pines for them, howling and lying by the door whenever Mum goes out in them, which isn't very often because he growls whenever she tries to put them on. I do love him. Stupid mutt.

Mum asks whether I saw Damian at school.

I lie, saying that I ignored him to make her go away.

She says, 'Good – you must keep your mystery with men.' Yawn. I know what's coming next. I count down in my head: Five, four, three, two, one . . .

'Do you know, in 18 years of marriage your father has never seen me on the toilet?' she says.

Yes, because you've told me five million times, Mother.

'Have I?' she prattles on. 'Well, did I ever tell

you that if he comes in to use the toilet when I'm in the bathroom I always look away?'

'Yes,' I say, 'but why bother? When Dad wees he sounds like a horse. You can hear him from the bus stop.'

She tells me to stop being so filthy and that Phoebe might hear. I can't believe my mother still fancies my father, especially now he's got a receding hairline. But she must do, because that's how Phoebe came along. She tells anyone who'll listen, 'Phoebe was a mistake [drum roll] . . . but she's the best mistake I ever made!!!'

Sigh. If I had a pound for every time she's said that, I could – well – pay for a nose job.

And what's that they teach us at school about contraception? If a 12-year-old can grasp what a condom is, I don't see why a couple of fortysomethings can't. Still, I'm glad Phoebe's here. She's funny and she's now riding round the room on Simon's back. I can't imagine life without her.

Fake illness so I don't have to go to school. Put talc on my face and pretend I've been sick by flushing the toilet four times. Turns out Mum's off work sick too. I tell her that she looks about 90 today and she turns away with a really weird look on her face.

Honestly, she really does need to get a sense of humour.

I tell her about Treasure and her gorgeousness and how I'm sure Damian fancies her.

Mum says being beautiful can cause you no end of problems.

'Oh well, you got lucky then, didn't you, mother?' I say. Again – no laughter. Lighten UP, woman.

Mum says I'm more fortunate than Treasure because she's an only child and big families are happier families. She's kidding – right? I'm blessed to sleep next to the Stink Pit?

I tell my mother that she is seriously misinformed. For a start, Treasure's dad is loaded and spends tons of money on her because he's always away working, PLUS her mother's given her a Topshop account card. She goes on three foreign holidays a year and doesn't come home from school to find that her little sister has made a hammock for Deirdre out of her best bra. Find me the bad bits in that, I challenge you. And what did we get? Two weeks in Gran's caravan in Wales where it rained for ten days without stopping and the showers had other people's front-bottom hairs in them.

'You've got a lot to learn about life,' says Mum. Er, well, she's got a lot to learn about what makes children happy.

After school, Amber brings round the home-work I missed. 'You got B minus for your essay about the Romans,' she says, looking disappointed for me. B minus? This is a personal best!

'Did anyone talk about me today?' I ask

'No, they were all gossiping about Natasha Marshall cos she had a love bite on her neck,' says Amber.

Saturday

10 a.m.

Am looking at my nose sideways in the mirror to see if it has grown any bigger. I think it has. Great. How long until they start calling me 'Beaky' and buying me Trill?

I've had a thought. Maybe I've imagined that Damian fancies Treasure. Maybe he's just being polite. Yes, yes, because he was nice to me too that day. Before, erm . . . the Poo Incident, which from here on will be known as the PI. My imagination has been getting carried away with itself again.

I make a list of 12 Solemn Vows, ways that I promise to be better if only God will make Damian like me instead of her . . . (yes, I know it's usually ten on these occasions, but I have a lot to atone for).

My Pact with God

1. I will go to church every Sunday (except when I'm on holiday, and when it's raining and I might catch a cold and when I actually have a cold. Oh, and when I'm having a sleepover at a friend's house, because I don't want them to think I'm some weird Jesus freak if I get up on Sunday morning and say, 'No, I don't want to go on Facebook with you and eat chocolate muffins. I'm off to listen to Father Michael talk about fish and loaves and stuff.').
2. I will never again hide the TV remote from my dad when he wants to watch the news so I can carry on watching *Hollyoaks*.
3. I will never again swap my packed lunch with

Kieran Campbell for two tubes of Mega Dust sherbet and a packet of Monster Munch and then tell my mother I had a nutritious meal.

4. I will definitely never eat meat again and I mean it this time. Amber says the world would be saved if we all stopped stuffing ourselves with cows and pigs. Not that it stops her.
5. I will not do Deirdre Disco Ball ever again. Nor will I let Phoebe dress Simon up in her old bonnets and skirts or give him a makeover with Mum's best eyeshadow and lipstick.
6. I will do my homework on time and only copy off Amber when it's science or maths. Or geography. And sometimes German, when it's the grammar bit.
7. I will not tell Rick's friends again that he watches *Sleeping Beauty* with Phoebe and sometimes pretends to be the handsome prince riding by.
8. I will not tell my mother I hate her because

she failed to wash my Daisy Duck top in time for the youth-club disco (although I wish to clarify that there really was no excuse).

9. I will help old ladies across the road and not get impatient when they don't move fast enough.
10. I will not complain that my nose is big because, hey, everyone's special in God's eyes.
11. I will not laugh when Andrew Slater calls Miss Jeffer, our PE teacher, Jeffer the Heifer just because she's what my gran would call 'well built'.
12. I, erm, will think of another one later . . .

I roll the list into a scroll, tie it with a hair bobble and put it under my bed.

6 p.m.

Gran comes round, fussing about her bowels again. 'I've been lovely and regular and then I stayed one night at Cissy's – just one night! – and my body clock's all gone to pot again,' she's saying to my mum in the kitchen. Why are old people like this? If we went on about our poo all day at school we'd get told off for being 'crude' and 'vulgar', but once you're past 70, it seems you can say what you like.

'How old are you, Gramma?' says Phoebe, who is for some reason painting her Barbie dolls' eyes black and white, like Marilyn Manson's.

'I'm 79 years young, love,' says Gran, like always.

'Oh,' says Pheebs sweetly, 'does that mean you'll die soon?'

6.30 p.m.

I know what will happen when I go down and say hello. 'Hello, Danielle – have you done your packet?' she will ask. 'Phoebe, Rick – have you done your packets?' She means have we done a poo today. She always asks this, even when people are here from school and I have to pretend she's talking about sending a parcel to an African charity or something. She really does need her head examining.

Remember I need to put Clearasil on my blackheads.

7 p.m.

That's funny – Mum and Gran are still murmuring in low voices in the kitchen and Mum hasn't even shouted up telling us not to be so rude and come down and say hello to our grandmother. I go into the kitchen. They stop talking immediately. 'Oh, hello, Danielle,' says Gran absent-mindedly. Not so much as a 'how are you?' She didn't even enquire after my packet! I am offended. Old people are so self-obsessed.

7.10 p.m.

It's meat-and-potato pie for tea, my absolute favourite, but I inform my mother that I am now vegetarian and that it's about time she started considering the welfare of animals too.

'Are you going to last more than two days this time?' she says.

I explain that this is a life decision.

'Well, you'll have to make yourself a cheese sandwich then.'

I hate cheese. I also hate vegetables. This is a problem. Maybe I will starve to death. Not that anyone will notice. But imagine how good that would look to Damian as my epitaph: 'She loved animals so much, she perished.'

Sunday

Mum decides we should all go to the park with Simon 'as a family'. Rick lies that he's got mocks to revise for so it's just the four of us. There's a bit of a kerfuffle when Simon ruins someone's picnic by running through the middle of it and stealing the sausage rolls, but after we've calmed Mr Angry Middle-Aged Man down it's quite a nice day all in all. Mum is still being a bit weird and emotional, saying to me and Phoebe stuff like, 'You're both still my babies, you know. Don't forget that!'

Dad rubs her like she's a distressed pony. Phoebe is outraged. 'I'm not a baby!' she says. 'I wipe my own widge.'

Monday

Drag Amber to the chemist's with me after school. Have decided that in order to make Damian see sense and prefer me to Treasure I am going to have to change my look. I spend £3.99 on a mascara that promises 'telescopic lashes to get you noticed!'

'You can't wear it for school,' says Amber, always the goody two-shoes. 'Mr Cook [the headteacher] will just make you scrub it off.'

'Look, if Treasure can get away with it, so can I,' I say. 'Now I need some tanning lotion.' Amber says it might be toxic and that I have no idea what I'll be putting on my skin and why don't we go home and research it on the internet first?

Honestly – what is she like? 'Everyone uses it,' I say, and at least I'm not going on one of those sunbeds that give you skin like an old tortoise. Except that I don't have enough money left for a whole bottle.

'Good, let's go home,' says Amber. But then I spot some little sachets of 'self-tan towelette' which cost 99p each. Amber thinks they'll be rubbish, but I tell her to shush and lend me a pound so I can buy three. I will apply it tomorrow when Mum is at the pub quiz with Auntie Karen.

Tuesday

Amber comes round at 6 p.m. to do the deed and we tell Dad we are going upstairs to do our history homework. 'I'm glad one of Danni's friends is having a good influence on her,' he says. Amber's face goes all pink and guilty-looking. She really is a hopeless liar.

Simon's head is resting cutely on his 'girlfriend'. When Dad tries to pull Mum's Ugg boots away from him he growls and buries them under his front legs like he's hugging them. They cost £100 and are now covered in slobber.

'It says you have to exfoliate first,' says Amber, squinting through her glasses at the packet.

'What does exfoliate mean?' I say.

'I don't know,' she says.

'Just ignore it then,' I say, and start taking off my school uniform.

'Are you sure Damian's worth all this trouble?'

she says. 'I sometimes think he seems, you know, a bit up himself.'

Poor Amber – she just doesn't understand boys.

I'm going to do my face and neck and Amber's doing my legs and arms. It just feels like one of those wet serviettes you sometimes get at the end of a meal in a Chinese restaurant. It says it will make me look 'tanned, healthy and glow with summer radiance' within 12 hours. Amber looks doubtful and says it seems a bit cheap. She's such an old woman, that girl. We rub it on and then I hear Dad bringing Phoebe upstairs to bed. She wants to come in my room, like always, to be with the big girls. I shove a T-shirt and some jeans on and tell my dad she can come in for ten minutes, tops, because we've got a lot of Roundheads and Cavaliers to get through, actually.

Phoebe plays with my pencil case, pulling things out and saying, 'I have this?' and, 'I keep this?' while me and Amber run round destroying the self-tanning evidence. Amber says she'd better be off home and scuttles out of the house. Honestly, she's such a wet sometimes.

'You smell funny,' says Phoebe, climbing on to my knee and sniffing my face like Simon does when I've got strawberry lipgloss on. It is true that the tanning towelettes do whiff a bit like smokey-bacon crisps, but that's not a bad thing, is it? I tell her to button it or I won't read *Room on the Broom* to her for the 472nd time.

Wednesday

7 a.m.

Wonder what I'll look like? I don't expect to look exactly like Treasure, but at least I'll be brown like one of those contestants on *Celebrity Love Island*. I look in the mirror in my room, ready to drink in my bronzed loveliness. OH. DEAR. GOD. ABOVE. It looks like I've turned into an elephantine rasher of streaky bacon. My face is striped like a bumble bee and my hands are so smeared it looks liked I've wiped my bum with them.

Luckily Mum is still in bed because she's tired – again – but Rick sees me when I go down for breakfast. 'Ha! You've been Tango'd,' he says.

I try covering it up with Mum's foundation cream, but the orange streaks show through. My dad says I could always pretend I was using Phoebe's wildlife face paints and it all went wrong. Phoebe, quite seriously, asks if I want to borrow her pussycat ears.

Dad seems to think this is hilarious until he realizes it won't wash off. 'Get to school before your mother sees you,' he says. I'll have to save the mascara for another day.

8.25 a.m.

I'm waiting at the bus stop wearing a duffle coat with the hood up and a scarf around my neck. It is almost June. Some kids from Year 7 ask me if I'm dressed like that for a bet. I tell them to go away, except I use a very bad word.

Can I just say here that Amber is no help? When she arrived she just kept staring at me saying, 'Oh girlfriend, that's so bad. SO, so bad.' Why does she speak like this too? Does literally everyone think they're American?

I decide I just have to tough it out before I melt and so I take off the coat and scarf and just sit on the bus miserably awaiting my fate. It comes in the shape of James Burgess from Year 9 who comes over and holds his hands up to my face going, 'Aaaah, that's toasty,' as if warming them against a fire.

'At least I haven't got a gap in my teeth you could fly a light aircraft through,' I say. He looks a bit chinned.

In school, everyone is gathering round me asking whether I've been burnt on a sunbed or had an allergic reaction to carrots. Ho, ho, how my sides are splitting. Then I see Treasure arriving with Damian.

'Oh Danni, you HAVEN'T been trying to put self-tanning lotion on yourself, have you? Oh, that's so sweeeet. But you should only ever have it done by a professional. Otherwise you'll end up looking like that – a big, smudgy mess.' Damian pulls her away.

Miss Judd comes in. 'What on EARTH has happened to your face, Dench?' she booms.

'It's, er, a fake-tan towelette that went a bit wrong, miss,' I say, knowing that this sounds quite funny. The classroom roars with laughter.

'Why you girls think it is attractive to have orange faces I will never ever know,' she says. 'Go to the headmaster's office.'

10 a.m.

I have been sent home by Mr Cook. Quelle result! Why didn't I think of this sooner? Planning to spend all day updating my Facebook page and watching CBBC. (I know – pathetic. Don't tell anyone.) Wonder whether I should buy a year's worth of tan towelettes as an investment. I could sell them at school.

3 p.m.

Mum comes home from work early after collecting Phoebe from nursery. She's so wrapped up in herself she doesn't even notice my face until Phoebe starts stroking my hair saying, 'Here, kitty, kitty. Naughty kitty need baff.'

Mum is quite angry that I've been sent home and sends me to lie in the bath for an hour with some of her essential oils. Another result.

6 p.m.

Amber comes round with Megan to cheer me up. Megan is my second-best friend but sometimes I promote her when I want to borrow her iPod/red jacket. We watch a DVD and then go to my room to sing on the Karaoke machine Dad got me from Argos for my birthday last year.

Megan, who wants to leave school and be a singer when she's 16, does *Born This Way* by Lady Gaga. I put on my mum's white high heels, shove two socks down my bra and do an impression of Treasure doing a Cheryl Cole song and tossing her hair. Amber and Megan are rolling round my bed laughing so much they nearly wet themselves. I should be on the stage really.

Dad shouts up that we have to turn it down and that other people live in this street too, and that if he wanted to listen to cats being skinned alive he'd prefer if it was those ones that use our garden as a toilet. He's such a self-centred man. Come to think of it, he's looking a bit old and careworn these days too, like my mum. Grumpy old pair of miserable boots.

I show Amber and Megan my Pact with God

to make Damian like me. They look at each other a bit funny.

'What?' I say.

'Nothing!' they say, in voices that are too high.

'If you don't tell me, I'll let Deirdre out,' I say (Megan has a fear of rodents).

That does the trick. She tells me that on Friday, when I was off sick, Treasure announced to a group of girls that she'd been to the pictures with Damian to see some stupid film in 3D and that they exchanged friendship bracelets. She kept getting it out and showing anyone who was walking past.

I stare at them. Feel super sick, like I've been kicked in the kidneys with a pair of wedges. Here's my advice to anyone who's interested – NEVER make a pact with God because He doesn't listen. In fact this is proof that God doesn't exist. There's no way I can compete with Treasure. She's pretty and has boobs AND an iPhone. To my horror and shame I start howling until big bubbles of snot come down my nose.

Mum and Dad come rushing up the stairs. 'For God's sake, what's wrong?' asks Mum.

'Damian's given Treasure a friendship bracelet,' I wail as tears run off my nose.

'Jesus, is that all?' says Dad. 'Lads your age are ten a penny – they're like s*** in a field.'

Megan and Amber start sniggering at this but I tell them it's not remotely funny or relevant to compare my heartache to cowpats.

Monday

Didn't sleep much. I keep my head down all day at school, pretending to have a cold. My eyes and nose are red from crying, or possibly all the soap I've been rubbing into my face. I hide in the library at lunchtime and don't go to the toilets all day, even though I'm bursting, in case Treasure is in there, touching up her make-up and holding court to her giggly, stupid followers. Her mum buys her Clinique 'invisible' foundation so the teachers won't know she's got it on. Can you believe that? My mum says she could get a full shop in from Asda for what that costs.

But then, just as the last bell of the day goes after French and I'm scurrying out of the main doors with Amber, I literally bump into Treasure and she drops her maths exercise book right at her feet. She is surrounded by her smirking, fawning Klingons.

'Danni, are you OK? You look AWFUL,' she says, in a delighted voice.

One of the Klingons repeats, 'Yeah, awful.' What a cow.

'I think there's an echo in here,' I say. 'Either that or we've got a very stupid ghost in the school. Anyway, it's probably just pneumonia – nothing serious.'

Treasure is smirking, knowing she has bracelet-power. So I pick up her book and say,

'Here's your maths book. Oh dear – only 11 out of 20. Still, I suppose you don't have much time for revision at night after you've scraped all that muck off your face .' Her face clouds over – well, as much as it can when it's bright tangerine – but then she sees Mr Cook in the distance and smiles falsely instead.

I'm thinking, Don't show me the bracelet, don't show me the bracelet . . .

She doesn't. Now I'm annoyed and thinking, Show me the bracelet. Show me the bloody bracelet. 'Well, I hope you feel better for Thursday,' she says. Thursday? Thursday? What's happening on Thursday? 'The youth-club disco,' whispers Amber. Oh NO. I'm not going. I'm NOT GOING.

6 p.m.

Go home and cuddle Simon. He licks my cheeks, probably wondering why they smell of pet food. Thank God for animals. Take him for a walk and he chases Fat Madge, the cat that lives at number 28. Her owner, Mr Robinson, who is also fat, tells me I should learn to control my dog. I tell him he should learn to control his pet's rations of Kitekat so it might be able to run a bit faster. He tells me I'm a cheeky little *beep word* and he'll have a word with my mum. Good luck with that, mate. She barely even listens to Phoebe these days.

Eat one miserable baked potato with baked beans for tea while my murdering family all have spaghetti bolognese. Cow killers. I must buy a 'Meat Is Murder' badge.

Wednesday

Sean O'Connor asked me today at school if I was OK. 'Why does everyone keep asking me that?' I snap back.

'Because you've hardly spoken for two days and normally you, erm, never stop,' he says, fiddling with his Lucozade bottle. Strange boy. The cheek of it though! I am quiet and mysterious, aren't I? 'Isn't a person allowed to be ill?' I say, flouncing off.

Thursday

Wake up to angry voices in the kitchen. Simon is in disgrace. So far in one morning he has chewed:

- one cushion from the living room (red)
- one lipgloss (mine, actually)
- a three-pack of Dove soap (he's definitely going to vomit)
- a talking Peppa Pig with pull string (Phoebe is inconsolable and has been promised a trip to the Disney Store to stop her squawking).

I, the beta child, have just been told, once again, 'That dog only brings stress to our lives. It's supposed to be your responsibility.' *It?* How rude. He is a pain but he's got a face like a teddy bear and his paws always smell of cheesy Wotsits. What more do they want? Plus – if there's a better laugh than taking Simon through a car wash (in a car, natch), then I'd like to know what it is. He thinks the giant brushes are monsters and has a fit trying to fight them.

Realize that thinking about this has made me smile. I feel a bit better now. Maybe I will go to the disco tonight. Yes, I'll make Amber and Megan come with me.

5 p.m.

I literally have not a stitch to wear. Mum offers to lend me something of hers. Thanks, Mother, but it's not OAP theme night. I put on the Tesco sparkly top and jeans and slap on some of Mum's most expensive foundation cream. That'll teach her.

10 p.m.

Why did I let Amber and Megan selfishly talk me into going to the disco? Treasure was there, flaunting her stupid bracelet and standing with Damian all night. She did look stunning, in a spoilt-brat sort of way. She was wearing a denim playsuit thing and there were loads of drippy girls oohing and aahing round her all night.

'She can be quite nice sometimes,' said Megan. 'She lent me her felt-tips in history once.' Well, pardon ME. I'm SO sorry to have misjudged her. Put the bleeding flags out. (Note to self: Megan the traitor is now relegated to backup friend.)

When I go to the toilets to reapply my Rimmel lipgloss (borrowed from Mum – I'm sure she'd have said yes if I'd asked) who should come in after me? Treasure.

'Oh, hi, Danni,' she says, in a treacly voice. 'Seen the bracelet Damian gave me?'

'Is it a shag band?' I say airily. 'You must have quite a few of those by now.'

I can see she's annoyed by this, but she laughs sarcastically instead. 'That's just about your level, Danni. Actually it's a commitment bracelet.'

Commitment? COMMITMENT? The word is 'friendship', you desperate, push-up-bra-wearing airhead.

'Aaah, sweet,' I say, in my best Not Bothered voice. 'I used to have one of those when I was in primary school.'

She is rattled by this. But she is determined to deliver her killer line. 'Who knows,' she says, so simperingly I could slap her, 'one day after we've been to university, maybe Damian will make it an engagement ring.'

I have gone red like a sweaty raspberry but I'm not going to let her know I'm jealous. 'Oh, I doubt that,' I say. 'Not when he sees what you really look like under all that slap. I bet your parents would barely recognize you underneath six inches of concealer.'

I must say that was a pretty good retort even for me. Treasure looks winded. 'Oh, go home and clear out your ferret or whichever filthy caged animal I've heard you keep in your Clampett bedroom,' she says. Yes, I think I came out the winner there.

Time to go home.

Sunday

My parents are in the kitchen again, whispering, not smiling. Why are they whispering? Why are they not smiling? Something's going on. Maybe they're splitting up! Maybe my dad's having an affair. Brilliant! Thank you, God! Oh, except no one would have him, not with his disappearing hair and jelly belly.

Rick, who has just come back from taking Simon for a walk to get out of the way of them, agrees with me that they might be having marital troubles, because he caught Mum crying in the bathroom but she pretended she had just poked herself in the eye putting in her contact lenses.

'She looks like a woman scorned,' he says. Then he thinks for a moment. 'Who would you live with if they split up?'

This is a good question. It's like being asked to choose between tuberculosis and appendicitis. Neither is very appealing. 'Dunno. Mum probably, because of access to her make-up and hair straighteners,' I say. 'What about you?'

'I'd go wherever the Sky box was,' he says.

It must be so rewarding having children.

I'd like to talk more about this with Rick but he's gone into the Stink Pit and won't discuss it any more because he's going out with his mates from his class and must get into cool and aloof mode, which mainly consists of ignoring me.

2 p.m.

Mum has gone out, taking Phoebe, who's asleep in the pushchair, with her. Not a thought for beta daughter, note. I suppose it could be the other way round. My mum could be 'carrying on with another bloke' as Gran puts it. Mum is still quite pretty in a Nolan Sister kind of way and does keep talking about having to get rid of her love handles. Very suspicious. When I mentioned the other day about needing £4k for my nose job when I'm 18 she fell about laughing, grabbed her thighs and said, 'If there's any spare money for cosmetic surgery in this house, these are getting hoovered out first.' Self-obsessed woman. She's too old for anyone to care much what she looks like any more. Her life's nearly over, whereas I still need to find love.

5 p.m.

Mum and Phoebe are back. Mum looks sheepish and says, 'We went shopping with Gran.'

'I got a Don Lewey balloon!' says Phoebe. She means John Lewis. It's come to this. We are so neglected that my baby sister thinks a free Sale balloon that's been tied to some vacuum cleaner in John Lewis is a treat.

Mum and Dad go and whisper in the living room as per usual, but then they realize Phoebe is holding Deirdre up at the kitchen window and a line of neighbourhood cats with saucer eyes are staring at her from the garden and licking their lips.

This is another of Phoebe's – and my dad's – favourite pastimes, especially when one of the cats leaps at the window and brains itself. Dad especially enjoys that and always says, 'Nice one, Pheebs – ten points.'

We are a deeply sick family.

Monday

8 a.m.

My mother looks R.O.U.G.H. Maybe she's been hitting the Tia Maria that Aunty Karen brought back from Turkey. Or maybe she's been out with her fancy man! She was missing for three hours yesterday and I bet Phoebe was asleep for most of them. Plenty of time to do The Deed. Ugh.

Mum is still in her candlewick dressing gown. I heard her saying to Dad, 'I don't know if I can do this, Dave. I'm so tired.' Do WHAT? Is living with Dad making her tired? If so, join the club.

Dad seems strangely unbothered that his wife is having a passionate affair and is reading the sports pages of the *Daily Mirror*. He says, 'It'll all work out for the best, you'll see.'

What will? *WHAT WILL BE FOR THE BEST?*

8.10 a.m.

Mum's in the bathroom and I need to brush my teeth with the new whitening toothpaste I made her buy from Superdrug. I knock on the door. Is she crying? She's certainly making a weird snuffling noise.

'I just feel a bit fluey,' she says when I ask what's wrong. She's a terrible liar, just like her husband. I'll have to go to school without brushing my teeth. Gross. Maybe I can beg a chewy off someone on the bus.

4 p.m.

Weird day at school trying to decipher my parents' untruths. I was sitting rocking my chair back on two legs as I gazed out of the window wondering whether it might be something else – like we're all moving to Scotland. I don't want to move to Scotland. It'll be cold and Simon won't like that and there'll be no Amber.

'Chairs have one, two, three, four legs,' Miss Judd said, bending down to touch each one in turn. 'Use them.'

Why are teachers so obsessed with how many legs chairs have? Everyone knows that story about someone falling over backwards and knocking their teeth out with their knees is a total myth. And here's another thing teachers never shut up about either. 'Do you put your feet on the furniture at home?' they say. But when you answer 'yes' because it's perfectly true, they tell you off for being cheeky. Explain to me the logic of that. I'd never be a teacher. What a pointless life.

4.15 p.m.

I tell Amber I need to talk to her and so we go to her house and sit in her bedroom, which is filled with posters about saving rainforests and pandas and remote tribespeople. Sigh. Not ONE picture of Robert Pattinson. It's not natural.

Unburden myself of my worries. Amber sneaks into her mother's bedroom to borrow a huge hardback book called Women's Health. It has a picture on the front of a middle-aged lady laughing while eating a salad. Why would anyone laugh if they had to eat a salad?

She looks through it and eventually says triumphantly, 'Thought so! Your mother is going through The Change.'

9 p.m.

Am sitting in my bedroom, feeling sick, trying to unremember all the things Amber read out from that book about The Change. It means a woman is getting old. Past it. Her periods stop, which must be a good thing, obviously, but there was other stuff which sounded disgusting and I don't really want to go there, to be honest. Basically it means she'll be getting greyer and moodier with creaking joints and hot flushes and maybe even a hump on her back. So if she does want to have an affair she'd better hurry up because no one will look twice at her soon.

9.10 p.m.

Worse – I've remembered that I agreed to let Amber help 'take my mind off things' by accompanying her on a protest this weekend against a new bypass or motorway or cutting down some woods or something. I forget what. Anyway, I only said yes so that I can tell everyone at school and Damian will see that I take an interest in the wider world and am so much more intellectual than Treasure. But let's face it – a Curly Wurly is more intellectual than Treasure.

Tuesday

8 a.m.

Rick is feeding Phoebe raisins for breakfast and telling her that they are dead flies. 'Yum, yum,' she says, shoving more of them into her mouth. Weird child.

He likes Phoebe much more than he likes me. I even see him kiss her head sometimes.

'Which is your favourite Disney princess?' she asks, as she does 400 times a day. Rick knows the drill here. We all do. None of us is allowed to pick Sleeping Beauty because she's Phoebe's favourite because she wears a pink dress at the end.

'Snow White,' he says. 'Oooh, but she's UGGERLY,' says Phoebe. 'She's got SHORT HAIR!'

Bitching at three years old, I ask you. I should let her loose on Treasure.

I whisper to Rick that Amber has a theory about Mum going through The Change. But he covers up his ears and runs from the room shouting, 'Shut up, shut up, you're repulsive!'

Boys are so immature. No wonder it's left to women to do all the hard work in life.

6 p.m.

Totally boring day at school except that Damian and Sean came first and second in the boys' 200 metres in PE and Treasure was jumping up and down like an overexcited cheerleader. I was embarrassed for her so I said, 'Treasure, if you jiggle your boobs much more you'll get two black eyes.' All the girls laughed, but only because they're all jealous that Treasure is in a B-cup already. Jammy cow.

I tried to hit the ball into her face during rounders but smashed it into the air instead and Megan caught me out. She was instantly demoted to third best friend.

Thursday

Megan is reinstated as second best friend. She is already on an official warning for swallowing helium gas out of a balloon in science last term and singing 'Livin' la Vida Loca' in a Donald Duck voice, but she excelled herself in Miss Judd's class today. She had basically recorded her cat miaowing on her phone and hidden it down her sock, and every so often she pressed it so it sounded like there was a cat in the classroom.

Miss Judd kept swivelling her eyes around the

room like a meerkat, then looking under the desks and in the cupboard saying, 'If this is a joke you are ALL in detention.'

You know when you know you can't laugh but that makes you want to laugh even more? I caught Damian's eye. He was shaking and had tears rolling down his face but he didn't look away. He smiled at me. He likes me again! Hope springs eternal. Miss Judd said she'd keep us all behind until someone owned up. So eventually Megan put her hand up and said, 'Miss, I admit it was my pussy.' Well, that was it – I just spluttered all over the desk and was told to go and stand outside until I calmed down.

Megan deserves deep respect.

Friday

Sean O'Connor asked me at school today how my dog was. 'Fine – why do you ask?' I said. I never know what's going on in his head. 'Just wondered,' he muttered. Strange boy. He never looks at you when he speaks.

Then he spluttered, 'I've got my dog now. Mitzy. I've had her two weeks. Her owners couldn't afford to keep her any more. Maybe they could play together some time.'

Now hold on a second, mister – I am NOT spending my free time hanging out with Shy Boy Sean. I'm about to say, 'Simon has a very busy schedule over the summer actually,' but then I realize – this could be it, the lucky break I have been waiting for!

'Sure,' I say, casually rubbing a spot of paint on the floor of the art classroom with my shoe. 'We could meet in the park. I'll get Amber to come along too and you could bring . . .'

'Who? Bring who?' says Sean a bit suspiciously for my liking.

'Oh, I dunno – erm . . . Damian?' I say as if it was just one name I had picked from many at random.

Sean looks a bit grumpy and says he doesn't think that's a very good idea after 'last time', by which I assume he means the PI. 'But I could bring my cousin Neil,' he says. 'He likes dogs and has got a pet gecko.'

Oh whoopidoo – a day out with the world's quietest boy and his lizard-loving geeky cousin. My cup runneth over. But it's too late. Before I can think up a decent excuse I've already agreed to meet up a week on Sunday. Sean can't do this weekend because Neil's busy with some project or other which I can't remember because I'd fallen into a coma by this point in the conversation. Yawn, yawn, yawn.

8 p.m.

Amber stays over at my house as it's the eco-protest/march/sit-in/whatever tomorrow and my dad's giving us a lift. Can't wait. Not.

We sit in my bedroom eating Nobbly Bobbly ice lollies and trying to make Deirdre jump over fences we've made from matchsticks. She's useless. She's just too fat, like a furry cheese barrel on legs. And she's not going to get any thinner if she keeps shovelling Nobbly Bobbly down her throat.

She holds it in her paws like a squirrel with a nut.

'If you could have three wishes, what would they be?' I ask Amber

She says, 'One – an end to pollution. Two – world peace.' And then, clutching her hand to her boobs (what there is of them) melodramatically, 'Three – true luuuurve.'

I'm surprised at this third answer. I was beginning to think Amber might be, well, not a lesbian, but just Not Bothered. When we were ten we made a pact that we'd go to the same university and when we get married we'd live in the same street so that we could still see each other every day, but just lately I've been suspecting that Amber isn't like normal girls. I try not to look surprised.

'Just because I don't fancy Damian doesn't mean I don't like boys,' she says huffily.

'How can you NOT fancy Damian?' I say. 'It's not humanly possible.'

'He's vain,' she says. 'I see him checking his

reflection in the windows all the time, flicking his hair back,' and she does this impression of someone in a shampoo advert.

I don't answer this because I too check my reflection in the windows all the time. Who doesn't?

Some of Rick's long-haired friends have called for him. I can hear them downstairs calling each other 'man' and 'bro' again. My dad finds this hilarious. They're trying to form a band with Rick on the drums. It's called – wait for it – 'Fast Track'. My dad almost died and went to heaven when they told him this. 'Fast track to the dole queue, more like,' he said, rolling around laughing in his chair.

Phoebe comes in holding Mum's make-up bag which she's stolen from her bedroom. She wants to give Amber a makeover. I tell her Amber doesn't wear make-up and to please go away.

'But why, Amber?' she asks. 'You might be pretty if you did.'

Phoebe's bedtime, I think.

11 p.m.

Mum and Dad are laughing in front of the telly. I'm in my room. Amber says The Change doesn't make you feel bad every day and that her textbook says it can be a 'new phase in life'. Will this new phase involve going to the supermarket more often? That's what I want to know.

Saturday

10 a.m.

Dad is driving us to the protest in our embarrassing two-tone car. 'What's this about again?' he says. 'It's to demonstrate our objection to the new bypass they're planning, Mr Dench,' says Amber.

'What's wrong with a bypass? Bypasses are good!' says my stupid father.

'Oh no, they attract more cars, which cause more pollution and they ruin the countryside, Mr Dench,' says Amber patiently, as if addressing a person with learning difficulties.

My dad points out – and he does have a tiddly-widdly point – that if we look around us carefully we might notice that we are actually travelling to this protest IN A CAR. 'I don't understand young people now,' he goes on. 'Environmental protests! Kids your age should be doing something useful, like robbing gas meters.' He seems to think this is hilarious. Amber and I don't respond.

As I get out of the car I pause and say, 'Dad? Is Mum going through The Change?'

He stares at me for about five seconds. Then he throws back his head and explodes with laughter. 'Oh, that's priceless, that is,' he says. 'That's really made my day.' I seriously think my parents are losing it.

10.30 a.m.

I've never seen so many unattractive people gathered in one place. Or face hair. And that's just the women. Amber has this glowy look about her, like those Jehovah's Witnesses who knock on your door and ask if you want to be saved. One boy with Harry Potter glasses has climbed a tree and unfurled a banner saying: 'The Earth is Yours. Save It!' He is also wearing a dreadful T-shirt with 'I'm a lean, mean recycling machine!' on the front. No, you're not, mate. You're a skinny, drippy wimp.

Amber is looking on admiringly. 'Amber, if you ever buy a T-shirt like that, then I must tell you that we can't be friends any more,' I warn tersely.

Then I spot another boy standing awkwardly at the foot of the tree. It is Shy Boy Sean. 'Hello,' he says, a bit embarrassed.

'What you doing here?' I say, astonished.

He gestures with his eyes up the tree to the nerdy glasses boy. 'I'm with him. My cousin Neil.' It is the geek in the T-shirt.

Hold on. This is the boy I'm supposed to be dog-walking with next weekend rather than Damian? Oh, my so-called life gets better and better.

'Hello, Neil,' Amber and I say together, shuffling our feet. All the while I am thinking I MUST NOT say Nerdy Neil, I MUST NOT say Nerdy Neil, because I can be a bit Tourette's like that. It turns out that Neil is starting at our school in September because he's had trouble 'fitting in' at his own school. Right, so he's been bullied then.

Amber has now shimmied up the tree too. There are eight people up there now, all chanting, 'I have a dream and it is green.' It's toe-curling, but Amber seems happy.

'If they like trees so much, why are they trying to crush one to death?' I whisper to Sean. He sniggers. I seize my chance. 'How's, erm, Damian these days?' I ask.

Sean instantly looks shifty. 'Fine,' he says defensively.

'I can't believe he hangs around with trashy Treasure,' I say as breezily as I can possibly manage.

'Well, if they're happy, it's up to them, isn't it?' says Sean, looking at me as though I'm the personification of evil. Lovely. So Treasure's now even got Shy Sean under her spell.

12 noon

I sulk for the rest of the day.

When Amber's dad picks us up she's buzzing like a mad wasp, telling him how they're now going to march on the council planning meeting (I mean, what are we – old-age pensioners?). Her dad, who fancies himself as a bit of a Bob Geldof, seems impressed. I sit in the back on my own, seething and hating Sean for being so nice about Treasure.

3 p.m.

We are in Amber's bedroom eating hummus, crisps and breadsticks. If anyone tried to snog us now, they'd die from garlic fumes.

Amber is still raving about the fact that she sat in a tree with some boring people. Oh, to be so easily pleased.

I tell her what Sean said and that I feel depressed.

Amber puts her hand on my back like she used to when we were little. 'Maybe you should play it a bit more cool with Damian.'

'What do you mean? I DO play it cool,' I say.

'Well, not reeeeeeally,' she says. 'You could try and be a bit less . . .'

A bit less WHAT?

'Obvious.'

OBVIOUS? I am not obvious! I am the queen of subtlety.

'Well, you could not copy Treasure so much and maybe not STARE at him quite so much. I think people have noticed.'

I know Amber thinks she is helping, but right at this moment I want to flick her very hard on the nose. I'll get her back one day.

Still, I practise my 'I'm not even looking at you' walk in the mirror. Amber says I look like I've been hypnotized by Paul McKenna.

Monday

9.30 a.m.

School. Time to put the 'I'm not even looking at you' walk into practice. Ooh, ooh, Damian is queuing with everyone in the corridor outside the maths classroom. Here goes. But I'm concentrating so hard on staring at the floor I walk straight into the wall. Slam. If this was a *Tom and Jerry* cartoon I'd have a flat face like a frying pan. My geography lever-arch file comes apart and the pages flutter everywhere.

I can hear two people laughing – oh, what a surprise. The sniggerers are Mickey the Thicky and Treasure.

'Oh Danni you're so CLUMSY,' says Treasure in a twittery, patronizing voice. 'You're like a baby elephant sometimes.'

I want to cry. I banged the bridge of my (huge) nose when I walked into the wall and now I can't even think of a cutting reply so I just sit on the floor with my throbbing conk, surrounded by pages about rainforests. I want to cry, but I mustn't under any circumstances. Where is Amber? This is all her fault for the 'too obvious' slur.

Then – salvation. I feel two pairs of arms pulling me up. Strong arms. And a smell of hair gel. It is Damian and Sean. 'You OK?' says Damian, as Treasure looks on, giving me the evils.

OK? I'm on the crest of a wave!

'Your, erm, nose is bleeding,' says Sean, offering me a tissue, which I hope hasn't been used because I'm stuffing it up my nostril. Damian says they'd better walk me to the sickbay. No, no – carry me, Damian! Like Mr Darcy.

Treasure, obviously sensing the electric attraction between me and Damian, dives in and stands over me saying, 'I'LL take her.' Bog off, Treasure.

I ignore her and carry on looking pleadingly at Damian. I consider pretending to faint in Damian's arms, but then Amber comes running down the corridor – her last class had been kept behind. All she sees is me covered in blood and Treasure standing over me, so she shrieks, 'What's happened? Oh my God, has she HIT you?'

'Has WHO hit WHOM?' bellows the voice of Mr Ince, our maths teacher. This just gets better! He orders Amber to go with me to see the nurse, and I can hear him taking Treasure aside for a grilling. As soon as me and Amber turn into the next corridor I stop her and start giggling. 'Did she hit you?' she asks, all shock-faced.

'No, I walked into the wall, trying to look non-obvious!' I say, and we both just fall apart laughing, me with little droplets of blood spraying from my nose.

The school nurse cleans me up and says I can go home if I want, but I choose to go back to class so that Damian can see how brave and ungirlie I am. Everyone gives me a round of applause when I go back in – apart from Treasure, that is – and I bow like I'm on stage, but not too low because it makes all the blood rush to my nostrils.

This has been an extremely successful day.

Friday

Last day of term before the summer holidays!!!

'All right, class,' says Mrs Shutterton in English, 'I have a question for you. Who can spell "discombobulated"?'

Oooh, and I have a question for YOU, Mrs Shutterton – who on the whole planet is ever going to need to write or say or type the word 'discombobulated'? You may as well ask us to spell 'blutitriollisticalenchortrasirpfgjhkkfarlt'. Remind me never to become a teacher . . . What a waste of time.

No wonder she gets called Mrs Sh . . . well, you can probably guess.

She's given us a book to read over the summer. I thought she was meant to be good at English. She should look up the meaning of the word 'holidays'. The book she has given us is *My Family and Other Animals* by Gerald Durrell. Amber is thrilled about this because it's about nature and geckos and bugs and things. I, on the other hand, am not thrilled. My family ARE animals. I live this book every single day.

Mum meets me and Rick from school, saying she will 'buy us a milkshake' to celebrate the end of the school year. A milkshake. How will we stand the excitement? If this is Mother's way of trying to show she is a good parent she gets zero out of ten. 'I just wanted to spend time with my big boy and girl,' she says, with moist eyes. It must be her hormones again. Give me strength. Rick's face is all twisted in a way that looks like acute pain but which I know to be mortification.

We tell our mother that if she does not call us her BIG BOY AND GIRL ever again we will allow her to take us for a Frankie and Benny's pizza.

Sunday

Ugh. Today's the day I promised to meet Shy Sean and Nerdy Neil in the park. How can I get out of it? I could say Simon has dog swine flu and cannot leave the house because he is infectious to other four-legged beasts. But I've got to take him for a walk anyway, and knowing my luck I'll bump into them and be exposed as a big, fat liar.

I ring Amber and tell her that she's got to talk to Nerdy Neil and keep him away from me. 'OK!' she says, surprisingly brightly. Text Shy Sean and we arrange to meet by the memorial stone in the park.

2 p.m.

Amber is here with a camera because she wants to take some photos of 'nature'. Seriously. Do you see what I'm up against? I can barely believe we're friends sometimes. We have nothing in common.

3 p.m.

We walk to the park. Simon pulls me all the way on his lead like a Scud missile. This is very undignified for me because it looks as if I am waterskiing but on a pavement. Sean is wearing combat trousers and looks slightly less weird than usual. I cannot say the same for his cousin, who is dressed like my dad when he's going to Homebase, in a checked shirt and cords. He also has hair like our milkman, who might be as old as 50. But at least he's got different glasses on today and doesn't look like that man who reads the news. Plus, he has at least got a kind, smiley face despite being an ocean-going nerd.

3.30 p.m.

Neil says he thinks Simon is 'boss' and should be in a TV advert because he's so cute. Well, I did say this boy has his good points. But he is a very poor substitute for Damian, who should really be here today. I can't see why Sean couldn't do me a favour and bring him along. I'm doing him a favour by allowing my dog to bond with his, aren't I? Aaah, bless, they do seem to be in doggy love though – sniffing each other's bottom, rolling around with their mouths around each other's throat and making growly noises. Sean looks a bit worried about this.

'Don't worry!' I say, all masterful and Dog Whisperer-like. 'It's called mouthing and it's perfectly natural. It's how they play.' Sean looks at me with big, impressed eyes. Mitzy, his collie, is very sweet and pretty, though obviously nowhere near as pretty as Simon.

Amber is earning some brownie points by chatting to Neil the Nerdmeister. He's examining her camera and coming out with words like 'shutter speed' and 'pixels'. Amber is actually doing a good job of pretending to be interested. Who knew she was such a good actress?

4 p.m.

Just to make conversation, and in the hope that he will mention it to Damian, I tell Sean that I am now a vegetarian. He looks impressed again. Or rather he just looks at me. Have I got a bogey on my nose?

5 p.m.

Oh God. Wish I hadn't mentioned the vegetarian thing. Neil, who has not eaten meat since the age of five 'because I don't eat anything with a face' offers to bring some leaflets round to my house. He wants me to sign up to the Vegetarian Society, Compassion in World Farming and all sorts of other things that I just don't have time for in my busy life. I don't mind having principles – I just don't want them intruding on my leisure time. Amber says that she'd like to see the leaflets though. Good. That's got him off my back.

'Where's Damian today?' I ask Sean as casually as I can manage.

'Gone on holiday with his family in France,' says Sean. Oh no – he'll come back with a tan and look even more gorgeous.

'But when's he back, when's he back?' I shriek, not at all casually. 'How should I know?' says Sean. Honestly, he's a very tetchy person.

Monday
11 a.m.

Aaah, a nice lie-in. And I deserve nothing less after my traumas.

Yesterday wasn't too bad, considering. The dogs loved it. Not that I'll ever do it again.

Just had a text from Sean suggesting that we do it again.

'Deffo!' I text back. Why can't I just say no?

Phoebe comes and starts tying Play-Doh ribbons into my hair. 'I got a boyfriend at nurthery!' she says. 'He kith me!'

What is wrong with me? Even my baby sister has a boyfriend, and she can't wipe her own back bottom.

Still, this is nice. Simon is in bed with me too, with his Ugg-boots girlfriend, which he has, rather disgustingly, buried under my duvet. He seems to have full-time custody of the boots these days. When winter comes and Mum remembers she quite likes wearing them I predict some shouting chez nous.

No school for six weeks. I could live like this forever.

Tuesday

Bored, bored, bored. I can't LIVE like this. No one can be expected to live like this. I could almost clean out Deirdre's cage, but I'm not quite that bored. This is what it must be like being Simon, sitting around the house all day but without even being able to text his doggy friends.

August

Thursday

It's my 13th birthday tomorrow, not that you'd notice, thanks very much. Here's a tip: never be born in August because there's no school so everyone's away on holiday and forgets about your birthday, even though you've attended their boring parties all year round AND given them presents. If you're unlucky enough to be born in August AND be a beta child – well, your life's basically a non-event. I'd better get the iPod I asked for, that's all I can say.

Friday

9 a.m.

I'm officially a teenager! Perhaps my parents will finally start taking me seriously and treating me like the intelligent young woman I am.

Go downstairs to the kitchen. Mum throws her arms around me.

'Happy birthday, my lovely little Danni-bear!' she says, thrusting a package into my hand. It is a pair of slippers in the shape of giant Dalmatian dog heads. This better be a joke.

'Pongo! Perdita!' says Phoebe, rubbing the footwear tenderly against her cheek.

'Awww, don't you like them, love?' says Dad, ruffling my hair. Thank God. Behind his back I can see a smaller parcel. I tear off the gold wrapping paper. Oh. It's an MP4 player. Not quite the Apple one I was hoping for, which costs considerably more. Oh, well. At least it's pink and quite a good one. I'll just have to hope Treasure doesn't mock it. I smile and say, 'Thank you! It's almost exactly what I wanted.'

'I can't believe it was only 13 years ago today that I was pushing you out!' says Mum. 'I've never known agony like it.' Oh, for God's sake, Mother.

Phoebe climbs on my knee. She has made me a card which features a picture of me (looking very fat, actually), Phoebe (like a beautiful princess, obviously) and Simon, all inside a big love heart. Bless her. She hands me a badly wrapped parcel. It contains a plastic Toy Story side plate (used) and a Jaffa cake.

Mum says she'll make me whatever I want for breakfast. 'Crunchy Nut Cornflakes,' I say.

'Ah, sorry – we've run out,' replies Mother dear.

Gran arrives. I open her present, which is the

same thing I get every year – £10 in a card and a Terry's Chocolate Orange. 'Oh, I don't envy you lot being young today,' she says. 'You couldn't pay me to go through all that again, with all life's pain and heartache ahead.' Oh, happy birthday to you, Danielle.

Rick, naturally, hasn't got up yet, but Mum says I can open his card. It's got 'To a great sister' on the front and, more importantly, a £15 Topshop voucher inside.

'Isn't that thoughtful of him?' says Mum.

'Mother – you bought the card and the voucher for him, didn't you?' I ask.

'Well, yes,' she says, 'but, look – he signed it!'

Oh, yes – I'm welling up here. But the good news is I get £20 from my Aunty Karen and another £20 from my godmother who lives in Wales. Result.

My parents are still being mysterious though – and today of all days. I heard Mum whispering to Gran before, saying something about appointments and how she and Dad will have to go off in the car later while Gran babysits Phoebe.

Maybe we ARE moving to Scotland. Well, I'm not going. Rick has said he won't go either because Fast Track needs him, and anyway he's 16 next birthday. We'll both have to live with Gran and spend 24 hours a day discussing our bowels.

2.p.m.

Because I'm not having a party – not enough people around – Dad has also given me £30 to take Amber and Megan for a pizza in town. Meet them under the big clock in the precinct. Amber has bought me two goats for some African village (sigh), but also some lovely bubble bath and soaps. Megan has bought me HMV vouchers and a lipgloss like the one I'm always borrowing from her. Hooray.

Even though it's MY birthday, Megan says she

wants to get a new skirt. I don't mind shopping: I do need a 'sizzling summer look' as it says in Mum's magazine, in case I bump into Damian at any point.

We decide to play our occasional game of trying on the most frumpy clothes we can find in Debenhams.

I pick a hideous flowery dress with an A-line skirt and Megan goes for some green old-lady cords. Then we see Amber looking a bit weird and we both suddenly remember that she wears green cords almost exactly like that, so Megan shoves them back quickly and picks some brown slacks instead. Amber has selected a grotesque long tulle dress like a demented Disney princess might wear.

We stand squashed together in the changing rooms. Megan looks like a fat farmer's wife in her slacks and Amber looks – well, quite nice actually. Bizarre.

I look brilliantly like an old biddy in my dress – in fact just like Miss Pye, our misery-guts deputy head who's about 90. So I do an impression, stooping a bit: 'Girls must NOT hitch their school skirts up to their thighs! It is vulgar and UNLADYLIKE. Anyone whose skirt is more than ONE INCH above the knee will be sent home. IS THAT CLEAR??' Amber and Meg are crying with laughter.

Suddenly the curtain is pulled back. 'How are we getting on in here?' says the changing-room assistant, a bit suspiciously.

'Great!' we say.

'Are you going to BUY any of these clothes, because if not can I remind you that there is a queue for these changing rooms?'

'*Heil,* Hitler,' I whisper. Amber and Megan snort again and so we're asked to leave. Where is the joy in life, eh?

Buy a new bag from Topshop but can't find anything 'hot' or 'sizzling' to wear, so go to Pizza

Hut instead. Afterwards we're still hungry so buy some chips which we eat in the precinct. It's been quite a nice day all in all.

6 p.m.

Amber and Megan are coming back for a birthday sleepover. Gran is making our tea: sausage and chips for everyone else, but veggie sausage (ugh) and chips for me and Amber. Is it illegal to have chips twice in one day?

Mum and Dad are still out. Phoebe has stolen one of Dad's work ties and is using it as reins as she rides around on Simon's back saying, 'Giddy up, Samson.' (Samson is the prince's horse in *Sleeping Beauty*). Rick is hogging the computer, probably uploading yet more pictures of himself on Facebook.

I say, 'Thanks for the Topshop voucher.'

He looks at me with not a clue what I'm talking about.

Amber and Megan go to my room and I slip into the kitchen for a quiet word with Gran.

'Gran, what's going on with Mum and Dad? They keep whispering and Mum's looking, well, quite ugly.'

Gran's face goes pinched. 'That's a terrible thing to say about your own mother! But, yes, I know what you mean. Anyway, it's nothing for you to worry about,' she says.

'Aha! So you do know then,' I say, pointing my finger in her face.

'You know me,' she says. 'See all, hear all, say nowt.'

You couldn't say 'nowt' if your life depended on it, I want to say, but instead bleat, with a tremble in my voice, 'Well, if we're moving to Scotland, I'm not going. I'm going to move in with you.'

She looks surprised. 'Scotland? Where did you get that idea?'

'Oh, OK, well, is Dad having an affair, then? Are they getting divorced?'

Gran puts her arms around me. 'Where do you get these ideas at your age?' she says. Then she looks all worried again. 'You'll find out soon enough – there's nothing you can do about it, put it that way.'

Oh yes, very reassuring, Grandmama dear.

8 p.m.

We are playing my new not-an-iPod. The phone rings downstairs. Gran answers. When she replaces the receiver she informs us that Mum and Dad have gone to the cinema for some 'quality time' together. That's lovely on your daughter's birthday!

Rick lifts his head up from the computer and shouts: 'It's a make-or-break date to save their marriage.' He's been reading Mum's *Closer* magazine again.

9 p.m.

We are watching TV in the living room when Gran gears up for her main enquiry. She asks after our packets. About time too. Amber and Megan are trying to stop themselves laughing but they're making snorty noises instead. Rick and I grunt that our packets are just fine. She also asks Rick whether he has a girlfriend yet. He tells her to shut up. That'll be a no then.

Saturday

Oh, deck the halls with boughs of holly. It seems that we are going en famille to Gran's caravan in Wales tomorrow for a couple of days. So just to recap: Treasure is in Italy, Damian is in Bordeaux and I am going to a campsite where they still use Izal bog roll.

Amber says it'll be better for our carbon footprint than a holiday to Spain. She'll get my footprint up her bum if she doesn't shut it.

Sunday

Two hours trapped in a crap car listening to *Charlie and Lola's Favourite and Best Music Record* while Simon makes record-breakingly pungent fart-smells in the hatchback. Ah, this is the life. Rick zones out with his headphones on.

'That dog stinks,' says Dad, opening a window. He can talk. Anyway, Simon's only rolled in one dead bird and some fox poo since his last bath.

6 p.m.

Drinking a rubbish cup of tea in the caravan's 'living room' area while Phoebe unpacks her miniature Dalmatians suitcase into the kitchen cupboards. Gran has the smallest caravan ever. It's ridiculous, designed for Oompa-Loompas. Rick nudges me. Mum and Dad are having a hushed row in the 'bedroom' area. They are doing that 'whisper shout' thing, but there's really no point since the walls are as thin as the Izal paper I'll no doubt be wiping my bum on later.

I'm sure I just heard Mum hiss, 'I just think they should know, Dave.'

'What did she say?' says Rick. 'Shhh,' I say. 'Listen.'

'Not yet,' says Dad. 'We don't know if it's going to work out yet, do we?'

'We can HEAR you,' shouts Rick.

Dad pokes his head round the door and smiles. 'Hear what? We're just discussing where to go tonight. Now – who's up for Bobby Beachball's?'

I'm getting bored with this guessing game now.

Bobby Beachball's is the dismal campsite 'family-entertainment nitespot'. In other words, it's a pub where grown-ups can take their children to watch rubbish acts while they get drunk. Me and Rick groan. Dad promises Rick a 'strong lager shandy' and this actually seems to cheer him up. God, his life must be even emptier than mine.

10 p.m.

Dad is tipsy. He has put his name down for the karaoke. Mum, because she has no shame, seems OK with this, but his three children, the fruit of his loins, are not. Phoebe is whining, 'Please no, Daddy,' while Rick and I are just disgusted. But it's too late. He's going up to the stage to do 'Let Me Entertain You'. This is a man who's 45, with the beginnings of a bald patch, who genuinely thinks he can pass for Robbie Williams.

Everyone's cheering, but his three children are, as ever, stony-faced.

When I get married to Damian we are never ever coming to a caravan park for our holidays.

Monday

12 noon

There is a vile child aged about five in next door's caravan. He's called Jake and keeps coming over to Simon to hit him with a stick while saying, 'Bad doggy.'

What I'd like to do is strangle the little brat, but instead I say, 'Don't hit doggy. Doggy might get cross and bite.'

'Yes!' says Phoebe, delighted to have an older kid to tell off. 'Bite your HEAD OFF.'

Jake stares at us, then runs away, but he's back two minutes later with a fishing net on a pole which he uses to poke Simon in the eyes. Simon yelps, then, quite understandably, growls.

'Do NOT hurt the doggy, you little horror,' I say angrily, snatching the fishing rod and 'accidentally' snapping it in two over my knee.

The horror screams. His mother, who's got tattoos on her arms and is a bit scary tbh, comes over.

'Wassgoinon?' she says.

'Shebustedmaaaaane-e-e-t,' wails the hell-child, pointing at the broken net. People in this family clearly cannot separate their words.

'It, er, snapped,' I say as casually as I can manage. 'He was hurting the dog.'

The woman gives me evils and leads her vile brat away.

Mum calls me and Phoebe in to help get the lunch plates out. Do you note the sexism here? She asks us, her daughters, not darling son Rick. As I'm wiping the ants off the side plates there's a huge scream.

Outside, Devil Boy is holding up his arm and crying while Simon has slunk under the caravan with his ears down. 'HE BITTED ME!' he's shrieking.

Then, as if in slow motion, all hell breaks loose. Devil Boy's parents are running over, Mum is shouting, 'He's bleeding! Has he had his tetanus injection?', Devil Boy screams even louder at the sight of his own blood trickling down his chubby arm, and I go wading in saying, 'It was his own fault. The little brat was poking Simon in the eyes!'

'I'm phoning the police,' says DB's father, glaring at me. 'That dog needs putting down.'

'It's your brat that needs putting down,' I shriek back, outraged. 'He's a trainee serial killer.'

Mum tells me to shut up in a really furious, hissing voice, then goes to get her first-aid box out and dabs the wound on the boy's arm with some pink liquid. 'Get Simon away from here,' she hisses at me. 'Take him for a walk, quick.'

The injustice of it.

12.45 p.m.

Walking along the cliffs, Simon's subdued because he knows he's done bad. My legs are shaking with fear. What if the police take Simon away? Surely they won't if I explain what happened. I have Phoebe as a witness!

1.15 p.m.

When I get back everything is quiet. I open the caravan door slowly and Mum and Dad are sitting at the teeny table waiting for me. Their faces are like thunder. I gulp.

'Do you realize how very, very, VERY serious that was?' says Mum in a scary controlled-fury voice. 'We cannot have a dog in the house that bites children. End of.'

I wail and bellow that Simon was being tortured, but Mum and Dad are weirdly poker-faced about it.

Turns out that Dad went over to Devil Boy's caravan and calmed them down. It was only a little nip on the fat of his arm, and the father wasn't that keen on calling the police because the tax disc on his car has run out. But we are going home tomorrow and they say Simon's got to sleep in a kennel in the yard because he might nip Phoebe. What an utter pile of rubbish. He'd never harm Phoebe. He thinks it's his job to protect her. He loves her nearly as much as his Ugg-boots girlfriend.

'No chance,' I say.

'It's that or the police station,' says Mum. I don't push it because I'm confident they'll get over it in a few days.

Tuesday

Back home. Mum doesn't realize I have just put the spare 15-tog duvet in Simon's kennel to keep him warm. Ha. Serves her right. Phoebe has made some curtains out of pink crêpe paper and stuck them up in the kennel to make it nice for him. We are both sniffling a bit.

Midnight

It is raining heavily. Simon is howling outside. I can't bear it. He can't understand why he's not lying on my bed. In his little doggy mind he feels he's been abandoned by his own family. I put the pillow over my head. I hate my parents even more.

Wednesday

6 a.m.

Phoebe comes in to wake me up. She's holding a towel. 'Poor Simon. He's wet,' she wails.

We tiptoe down. Simon has his head on his paws looking forlornly out of his kennel prison. We run to him and he goes mad with joy, licking our faces and doing little happy whimpers. We let him in the house and I open one of Dad's favourite Fray Bentos steak-and-kidney pies for him. Ha! You'll pay for your cruelty, Father.

9 a.m.

I am mainly ignoring Mum and Dad, not that they seem to care. Beta child's distress is as nothing to them.

12 noon

Take Simon and go and meet Amber in the park. She is outraged by the treatment Simon is receiving and says we should start a Justice for Simon campaign. She's been talking to Nerdy Neil on Facebook and he knows someone who can get T-shirts printed with any slogan you want.

'Mmm, that explains the "Lean green recycling machine",' I snigger. 'Maybe he could get another saying, "A blind butcher cut my hair!"'

Amber doesn't laugh as much as I expected at this. Is it the law that if you care about the environment you must have NO SENSE OF HUMOUR?

2 p.m.

We buy chips for Simon from the park cafe. He seems to have perked up a bit, because he runs off and cocks his leg on someone's wicker picnic basket. Me and Amber hide behind a tree convulsed with giggles. Then we tiptoe out through the park gates with Simon running behind. Hooray – I don't think the picnic people realized he was with us.

11 p.m.

Simon is howling in his kennel again. Dad shouts, 'Shut up, mutt!' which makes him cry even more. I put the pillow over my head because I just can't bear it. Phoebe comes and gets into my bed.

She has drawn a picture of Mum and Dad in jail. 'Bad Mummy and Daddy,' she says.

Good girl, you're learning.

Thursday

Progress. Mum says Simon can sleep in the kitchen because the neighbours have complained he's keeping them awake with his howling. She is weakening. He'll be back in my bed by the weekend.

Friday

Megan texts me to say that she saw Treasure shopping with her mum in town. She's back from Sicily with a tan to die for. She's also had her hair braided and had a henna tattoo on her arm. That's against school rules, actually. I'm going to tell.

'Did she mention Damian?' I ask, as the sick feeling rises in my stomach.

'Only about 450 times,' Megan texts back.

Saturday

Sneaked Simon into my bed. Maybe the crisis is over.

Monday

The crisis is not over. Mum's just found the spare duvet in Simon's kennel. She goes so absolutely ballistic that Dad actually has to tell her to calm down. 'Things are going to have to change around here young lady,' he says to me, shaking the dog-hair-covered duvet at me.

Rick and two of his lanky new band friends walk in right in the middle of the screaming match. Rick looks at us with contempt. 'Sorry, dudes,' he says to his friends. 'My family are idiots.'

Dudes? What a loser.

Tuesday

Mum has bought Phoebe a sticky glitter pack as a reward for being a good girl at nursery. She is trying to give Simon a makeover with it and wants me and Rick to hold him down so he can't escape. Rick won't because he's just got ready to go out and is waiting for the lanky boys to call so they can go out together and make more rubbish music with their rubbish band.

I know that I vowed in my Pact with God not to do any more Simon makeovers, but God hasn't exactly delivered the Damian goods, has He? I get Simon on his back and put a knee on either side, holding his head while he tries to kick me off. Phoebe is painting his floppy ears with glitter paint. Just then the doorbell rings so Simon is barking, while trying to kick me off, while Phoebe paints his ears. When I look up, standing in front of me is Damian.

Hold on – DAMIAN!? In our smelly living room with the vomit carpet?

'You don't mind if my little brother comes along with us, do you?' one lanky boy is saying to Rick. 'Mum can't pick him up for an hour.'

You mean the boy that's been visiting our house these past three weeks is Luke, Damian's older brother?? For God's sake, why didn't Rick say??

Damian is silent. He is just staring at me straddling a struggling mongrel on my knees while a four-year-old paints its ears sparkly blue 'because he's a boy!'

They all leave. I stare at the door with my mouth in a perfect O shape.

Will he tell Treasure? That is the question.

Wednesday

Go for a sleepover at Amber's house. Can you believe her mum and dad only let her watch one hour of telly a day? That is what I call a deprived childhood. They only had one child, Amber, because they believe the world is overpopulated as it is. Tell that to the woman down our road who's got nine kids.

Amber's mum makes grilled organic chicken, steamed broccoli, organic mashed potatoes and peas. Amber has forgotten to tell her mother I'm a vegetarian but says I can probably still eat it because the chicken was organic and thus had a happy life. I think she has a point. Plus, I'm starving.

8 p.m.

Amber gets a text from Nerdy Neil asking her to suggest to me that we all meet up again.

'Oh, this is terrible,' I say.

'What is?' says Amber.

'Well, it's obvious – the Nerdmeister FANCIES me.' I sigh.

'Of course he doesn't fancy you. Don't be silly,' says Amber a bit sulkily.

Look – it's hardly my fault if weird boys find me irresistible, is it?

September

Thursday

12 noon

In my bedroom painting my toenails Scarlet Lady red and doing my face-workout exercises to ensure I never get wrinkles. It involves doing a lion face like a roaring beast and sticking your tongue out to your chin as far as you can with your eyes wide open. If Damian saw me now, he'd never marry me.

1 p.m.

Four days until school starts again. Suppose I'd better start reading *My Family and Other Animals.*

1.05 p.m.

On second thoughts, I could just get Amber to tell me what it's about. Busy people don't have time for books.

Feel a wave of sickness at the idea of starting school. Mental torture will resume. Plus Mum has bought me some hideous new pleated school skirts from ASDA! I bet Treasure's school skirts aren't from Asda. It'll be John Lewis or Marks & Spencer or more likely Harrods.

1.30 p.m.

The house is spookily quiet. Rick has taken Simon out and Phoebe is at Gran's. Hold on, what's that noise? It's Mum and Dad whispering. I listen at the bedroom door. What's Dad saying? Something about a hospital appointment? Who's going to hospital? 'Tomorrow at two,' says Mum. 'I'm scared, Dave.' Then she starts whimpering like a child while he makes shushing noises.

Oh my God, she's ill. She's really ill. And it's my fault. The stress of being my mother is killing her.

Maybe it's Alzheimer's. Or cancer. Oh dear lord, is it cancer? I fling myself down on my bed with a boulder in my throat. I do love her, even though I'm her third-favourite child and she never does the shopping. We couldn't manage without her. Dad doesn't even know how to bleach a toilet. Or switch on the washing machine (which has been broken for three weeks, by the way).

I hear her snuffling in the bathroom. I go in and put my arm round her and this for some reason makes her cry even more. My heart is beating really fast. This is scary.

'It's OK, love, I'm just feeling a bit poorly,' she says.

'Poorly with . . . cancer?' I blurt out, and I start blubbing.

Mum looks amazed, then sad, then a bit sheepish. 'Is that what you've been thinking all these weeks?' she says, giving me a hug. 'My poor little lamb.'

(Well, no, actually, mother. First I thought Dad was having a bit on the side and then that you were having a bit on the side and then that we were moving to Scotland and it's only today that I thought of cancer, but I want to milk this sympathy for all I can get.) So I just nod silently with big, red eyes.

'No, I promise I haven't got cancer,' she says, then shouts to Dad 'Dave, we're really going to have to talk to these kids. But not until tomorrow.'

Tomorrow? Oh, lovely. Prolong the agony, why don't you?

Still, she hasn't got cancer. Hooray! I'm not

going to take things for granted any more. I'm going to change. Because I totally love my mum.

Friday

3 p.m.

Can I just say that I totally hate my mum?

She is a disgrace.

None of us can look at her, except for Dad, who keeps patting her tummy proudly and saying, 'Sharp shooter, eh?' Whatever that means.

They called us all into a room – me, Rick and Phoebe – and then said, in nervous fluttery voices, 'We've got some very, erm, big news.'

My mother, aged 44 – practically a pensioner – is PREGNANT. Again! Can you believe it? She'll be 103 by the time she gives birth to this one. She'll be on the front page of the papers and there will be TV crews camped in the garden doing stories on Britain's Oldest Mother and then we will probably be taken into care because our parents clearly cannot control themselves.

Gran is appalled. The phone has just rung and I picked it up and it was Gran saying, 'Have they told you? Have they told you?' She says if my other grandma was alive she'd be appalled too, but as she's been dead six years it probably won't bother her very much.

Gran says my dad should have more self-control at his age (my thoughts exactly, Grandmama) and she can't imagine what they'll say down at the One O'Clock Club. She says we can't afford another mouth to feed and she hopes they don't expect her to babysit. Much as I agree, I know that my Gran will be cooing over this baby like a mother pigeon just like she was with Phoebe, so I can't really be bothered discussing it with her.

Mum went for a scan yesterday to check everything was OK with the baby. They couldn't be too sure at her age apparently, and she was petrified. But it seems fine. I'm astonished it hasn't got three heads. They showed us a picture of the scan where you can just make out a white blob.

Phoebe saw it and started crying, saying, 'Mummy's eaten a SLUG. Quick, get doctor.'

The baby is due in December, just in time to ruin everyone's Christmas. Well, isn't life turning out just peachy?

11 p.m.

What are we going to do? Rick says we should leave home asap because there'll be no room for us soon and the place will stink of baby sick again. He's gone out to lose himself in Fast Track.

I'm more worried about what Treasure will say when she finds out. The Clampetts have really done it this time.

Saturday

Phoebe now seems pleased about the baby and has given Mum all her Baby Annabel clothes. This made Mum cry like a banshee and rock Phoebe on her knee, saying, 'Mummy's lovely little baby.'

Enjoy it while it lasts, Pheebs. Soon you'll be joining the ignored-middle-children club.

Sunday

Unbelievable. Mum is actually looking quite happy about being pregnant now. She literally has no shame. And Dad keeps singing 'Isn't She Lovely?' and kissing her in front of her disgusted children. 'What would I do without you, Dave?' she says to my dad.

'Dunno,' says Rick. 'Not get knocked up at the age of 44?' Dad didn't laugh at that.

Text Amber and say I need an emergency summit meeting.

4 p.m.

Amber's bedroom. Summit meeting.

Amber stares at me with her mouth in one of the shapes in the Face Workout book when I tell her. I make her swear not to tell anyone, not even Megan, who can be very gossipy, to be honest. I was hoping Amber would join in agreeing what selfish, embarrassing parents they are, but she went all nerdy scientist on me, saying, 'Well, that's interesting actually, because it shows how incredible human biology is.'

'WHAT?' I said.

'Well, women's fertility drops quite sharply in their thirties, as does men's,' she said. 'Both your mum and dad must be quite—'

'All right, all riiiiiight,' I say, covering my ears and feeling that I really might be sick at any moment. Too much information – unless you want vommed Monster Munch all over your shoes.

Still, I must get home. I need to wash my hair with Mum's expensive shampoo and get my beauty sleep to look nice for Damian. I am going to start putting ME first in this family.

Monday

4 a.m.

Can't sleep. Am half appalled about the baby, half demented with excitement about seeing Damian again. Am going to wear my 'telescopic lashes' mascara so that when he looks into my eyes he realizes where his heart really lies.

5 a.m.

Still can't sleep. Because I'm panicking about not sleeping I can't sleep even more. Plus Deirdre is on her squeaky wheel. Shove her cage in the bathroom.

7 a.m.

Why, why, why did I lay awake for three hours? I now have huge black shadows under my eyes like a drug addict and my hair is a big mad crow's nest. I look like that batty old woman down the precinct who talks to herself and wears all her clothes at the same time.

7.30 a.m.

A piercing scream from the bathroom. Deirdre has escaped from her cage and nibbled Mum's feet while she was having a wee. Well, at least Deirdre's got one experience up on Dad who, as we know, has NEVER seen Mum have a wee.

7.45 a.m.

Lying on my stomach in the bathroom trying to coax Deirdre out from under the bath with a box of raisins. I so don't need this. I need to be getting SEXY.

8.10 a.m.

Deirdre now caught. I am now late.

Time for damage limitation. Sneak into the bathroom and squirt myself with Mum's Sarah Jessica Parker perfume. It is called Lovely. What a totally rubbish name. And not strictly true. They'd have been better off calling it 'Not Bad But A Bit Claggy'. I squirt tons of it on. It's not as though Mum will be needing it again, since she won't be going out for the next 100 years.

Apply my telescopic mascara. You're supposed to let it dry between each coat but it won't matter.

Not bad actually. Apart from the red eyes, which look like raw liver.

8.20 a.m.

Phoebe is dressed in her nurse's uniform and is holding up an old stained bib to Mum's tummy saying, 'Hello, baby – you have dis.' She has also offered the fetus a tin opener and a dishwasher tablet.

8.30 a.m.

Meet Amber and Megan at the bus stop. Megan has been to Sardinia. Is any more evidence required that I am a disadvantaged child?

9 a.m.

New form teacher for Year 9, Mr Clough. He is into bodybuilding and is wearing a short-sleeved shirt so that we can all see his biceps. How very sad. He must be nearly 40. Talk about midlife crisis. He'll be growing a ponytail next. He also calls us all by our last names as if we are in the army. Somebody should tell him it's not 1953, probably the year he was born.

Treasure is in the corner surrounded by people. She's handing out holiday presents to her coterie of sucky-uppy friends.

It's worse than I feared. She's still wearing the bracelet but also has a) a tan to die for, b) brand-new highlights in her hair, c) her ears pierced twice. Why aren't I allowed to have my ears pierced even once? Mum says it looks trollopy, but she's got three holes in each of hers, so what does that make her? An old trollope, that's what. Treasure says, so that I can hear, that her dad has bought her real diamond studs. 'Think how many starving African children you could feed with that,' I say to Amber as loud as I can.

Still haven't seen Damian.

10.30 a.m.

Chemistry. My legs are literally wobbling. They're like Bendaroos. We're lining up in the corridor outside the chemistry lab. Any minute now I will see him. Amber digs me in the ribs with her skinny elbow. 'Ow!' I say. 'There he is,' she hisses. If it's possible, he's even more gorgeous than I remembered. He's got a fading tan and his nose is peeling in a really attractive way. Alongside him is Sean – no tan, and no attractively peeling nose – but at least he's let his hair grow a bit so he looks older than seven.

'All right, Danni?' says Damian.

What? He said 'All right?' to me! And he said my name! Was it in a polite way or in an I'd-like-to-get-to-know-you-better way?

Amber, who always rains on my parade, says, 'No, it was a you're-blocking-the-classroom doorway-and- grinning-like- a-hyena-into-my-face-so-I-can't-exactly-pretend-you're-not-there way.'

Sean said hello too but I barely noticed. Trailing behind him is new boy Nerdy Neil. Amber is friendly to him, which is nice of her.

Damian is still wearing the bracelet. That is against school rules, actually.

I open my big pencil case and find that half my felt-tips have been stolen and been replaced by a Toilet Duck. Everyone is killing themselves laughing. Phoebe will pay for this.

2 p.m.

Ugh, PE. A chance for Treasure to show off her long tanned legs. At least I'm well better at games than her. Bet she doesn't like catching all those rounders balls in case she breaks a nail. I am bowling. Can't wait till it's her turn to bat. Would it be wrong to accidentally break her nose?

Oh, surprise, surprise. Treasure is trying to get out of games. She's telling Miss Jeffer that she feels ill.

'Maybe those holes in your ears are infected,' I suggest helpfully.

Treasure flashes me a dirty look and says sarcastically, 'Oh Danni, you seem to have a pair of tarantulas sitting on your eyelids.'

Miss Jeffer is staring at me. 'Danni, how many times do you need to be told that girls are not allowed to wear mascara for school. How much have you put on – a whole tube??' Damn, damn, damn. Now I'll be sent to scrub it off.

2.15 p.m.

What do you think happens when you try to remove mascara with those rubbish, tiny little cheap soaps they have in school? I'll tell you – it smears the black all over your face and makes your eyes sting. I now look like something out of the 'Thriller' video (God rest Michael Jackson's soul). Five hours in and I hate school already.

3.30 p.m.

Sean, Nerdy Neil, Damian and another boy, Matt, are at the school gates waiting to walk home. I'm a woman who needs to take charge of her life. I'm going to walk out with them. Grab Amber, who for once seems fine to go along with it.

'Hi – good holidays?' I say with the winning smile I've practised in the mirror but that Rick says makes me look constipated. Damian grunts a yes, Matt says nothing, but Nerdy Neil pipes up enthusiastically, saying, 'Hello, Danni. Great to see you in the park the other day. Let's all get together again soon with the dogs.'

Oh nooooo. He's making it sound like we're going out together or something. Damian will think I'm spoken for.

Sean looks embarrassed, as usual, so I say with a nervous laugh, 'As long as you don't bore on all day about saving the planet.' Neil's face kind of crumples like an old jumper. Oh dear

God, he does fancy me. Sean flashes me a dirty look – oh, for goodness sake, it was only a joke. Why does everyone I know have zero sense of humour?

Then I see Treasure wiggling out of the front entrance. She comes up and links her arm into Damian's like a cat spraying its territory.

'Ooh, Danni, you've got black rings around your eyes where you've tried to rub your mascara off!' she says in her high-pitched, girlie voice. 'You look like a panda. A pasty little panda!'

Damn, I meant to go back to the toilet and get some more paper towels but I forgot. Damn, damn.

Keep your cool, Danni. 'Oh well, we're all individuals, Treasure,' I say. 'For instance, if I wanted to look like you, I'd simply slather my face in the creosote my dad uses for the garden fence.'

Treasure flashes me a look of pure hatred. Then she does her really annoying twittery laugh. 'Oh, that tiny thing at the front of your house is a GARDEN, is it? I thought it was a junkyard. A very SMALL junkyard.'

Tears prick the corners of my eyes. Why does she always attack my family? And why can't Dad move that rusty bike? I never slag off her mum even though she looks like a WAG. Wait until she hears about my mum. I'll have to change schools.

'Come on, she's just vile,' says Amber, pulling me away and giving Treasure one of her baddest stares. Damian trots behind Treasure like an adoring Labrador.

Wednesday

There is a new school craze called 'Strike'. You creep up behind someone and put one hand on either side of their mouth, then pull their lips back into a horizontal stripe while shouting, 'Strike!' It's a blow to your dignity, to be honest, looking like a giant salamander. Obviously about five people have already done it to me, but NO ONE's done it to precious Treasure. I whisper to porky Laura Birkdale that she can have a stick of my Twirl if she'll 'strike' Treasure. She does! For two precious seconds Treasure looks like a trout! I now love Laura Birkdale even though she breathes really noisily through her mouth.

'Watch it, Laura,' I say. 'You'll need a trowel to get all that lipgloss off your hands.'

Friday

Damn, blast and pig poo. There's a geography field trip on Monday and the teachers say that as a special 'treat' we can wear our own clothes. Gee, thanks teachies. Treasure will wear something stunning while I, as usual, will look like a scarecrow modelling last season's George@Asda. I've only got three days to come up with a practical yet glamorous and back-to-nature outfit – sort of Angelina Jolie – so that Damian will see that I am the woman of his dreams.

Saturday

Mission this weekend: make Mum buy me new clothes. It's the least she can do, seeing as she's ruined my life. I approach her in the kitchen as she's giving Phoebe scrambled egg. The minute Mum's back's turned Phoebe is shoving it into Simon's mouth with her Dora the Explorer spoon, then licking it. Sigh. What would Treasure make of this Clampett cameo?

This is how the conversation goes:

Me: 'Mu-u-u-m, there's a geography field trip on Monday. I need something new to wear.'

Mum: 'Like hell you do. Old cords and a pair of wellies. That's what we always wore. Wear those blue ones from Primark.'

Dad (ever the joker): 'And I'm sure your Gran's got some Crimplene slacks she can lend you.'

Phoebe, smearing Simon-infested egg across her face: 'Not Iggle Piggle wellies. Dey mine!'

Me (panic rising/whiny voice): 'But, Mum, NO ONE'S wearing wellies. It's not 1978. Everyone else will be getting new outfits. I've needed new jeans for ages anyway. Can we go to Urban Outfitters, pleeeeese?'

Rick, walking in scratching his crotch, having just got out of bed: 'She'd better not be getting new clothes when you said I can't have new football boots. It's not fair.' (Is Rick six?)

Mum: 'Nobody's getting new anything! I'm not buying clothes for you to tramp around a field in, Danni. There's no spare money at the moment, now the new baby's coming.'

Me (even higher whiny voice): 'But why not? It's not OUR fault you're having a baby. And anyway – since when do babies eat caviar and champagne?'

Mum, looking guilty: 'Subject closed.'

I run out of the kitchen shrieking, 'I hate

you!' as Simon begins to lick egg directly off Phoebe's face. In my room I look through the collection of rags in my wardrobe and vow that no daughter of mine will never be so badly treated.

Sunday

Me and Rick are watching repeats of *Waterloo Road*. Rick can be all right when he's not with his mates. He says Liam, Damian's brother, thinks Treasure looks like a Bratz doll. Hahhahaha! I am LIKING this boy.

Dad comes in to ask if we want to go ten-pin bowling. Aha. They are creeping round us!

'No, ta,' says Rick.

'Why not?' says Dad.

'Because I'm not eight years old. I like football but I have no BOOTS.' He turns back to the telly.

Dad looks chinned. Ha. That will teach him to neglect his first-born children.

2 p.m.

Field-trip-outfit crisis deepens. Can't find my vintage Blondie T-shirt, which was my fall-back option. Will now have to wear leggings and a stupid gypsy top, which gapes because my boobs aren't big enough.

Text Amber to ask what she's wearing tomorrow. 'Old cords and wellies, obviously,' she replies.

Is Amber a pensioner in a 13-year-old's body? Discuss.

Monday

My gipsy top is a shamer. Shove a pair of Phoebe's Tinkerbell socks down my bra to fill the gape. Have a horrible feeling they're not clean.

9 a.m.

We're all gathered in the front courtyard at school, where the coach is waiting, so Mr Firth, the geography teacher, can take the register. Ugh, he's wearing 'leisure clothes' and SANDALS! Is there anything sadder than the sight of teachers in their 'weekend' gear? Miss Judd has actually chosen to wear red three-quarter-length trousers that make her legs look like chunky KitKats and – wait – a SCRUNCHIE! Even Phoebe turns her nose up at scrunchies, and she sometimes wears a sieve on her head.

9.05 a.m.

Treasure's late. Maybe she's sick. I can have Damian to myself all day! Hooray. Hoist my sock-boobs up a bit.

9.10 a.m.

Treasure's here, the witch, making a grand entrance in her dad's black BMW. She walks slowly towards the coach so we can all take in the full amazingness of her outfit. Tight white pencil skirt, pink (low-cut) top, a TRUCKLOAD of make-up and pink heels. Hold on – pink heels? For a geography field trip? 'She looks like an air hostess,' whispers Megan. As she walks down the coach we all say together, 'Doors to manual.' The teachers are too busy fussing over taking the register to notice her clothes.

Damian has saved her a seat. Pass the sick bag. Amber says he's a 'metrosexual'. I force a laugh even though I don't know what it means.

9.45 a.m.

Mr Firth gives us the usual spiel about behaving ourselves when we get to these boring rocks or wherever it is we're going. 'You must behave like adults' – yeah, got that. 'You are representing the school . . .' blah, blah, blah . . . Hurry it up, Firthy, some of us need a wee.

10.30 a.m.

There is light drizzle and we are standing in a field full of cowpats. And this is educational how? Treasure's skirt is so tight she can barely walk and has to totter holding on to Damian's arm.

'She looks like she's got worms,' whispers Amber. Sean hears and we all snigger. Miss Judd finally clocks Treasure's outfit as she hobbles across the field – and goes completely mental. 'Treasure, you were told quite clearly in your letter that this is a school lesson NOT a fashion show. Why didn't you wear flat shoes like everyone else?'

'With a pencil skirt, miss? You must be joking,' she says, checking her make-up in a pocket mirror.

And then something brilliant happens. Miss Judd marches back to the coach and returns holding some manky tracksuit bottoms and horrible cheap black wellies from the lost-property box. She orders Treasure to go behind a bush and put them on. Oh, I love field trips!

Treasure is stuttering, 'B-b-but I can't wear them, miss. They've been worn. And they're HIDEOUS!' But Miss Judd says it's either that or sit on the coach alone doing homework. So Treasure trudges off to the bush with a face like a slapped bottom.

'Is this next season's look then, Treasure?' I say when she comes out. 'Bag-lady-in-the-precinct chic?'

'Mmm, yes, these ARE disgusting clothes from lost property, aren't they?' says Treasure bitchily. 'Are you sure they aren't YOURS, Danni? Oh no, you're right – they can't be. They're not covered in dog hairs.'

I hate her.

Lunchtime

School fight

After we've measured some rainwater (yawn) and eaten our packed lunches while trying not to look at the cowpats, we go to the nearest village where Mr Firth says we can have 30 minutes' free time looking at the shops. Whoopidoo. So that's one wool shop, one second-hand bookshop, two places selling nothing but cagoules, and a Spar. Everyone runs to the Spar.

Me, Amber and Megan buy five jelly snakes each and go for a walk. 'Did you notice that Sean and Neil kept staring at us in the field?' says Megan.

'Mmm. Don't say anything, but I think Neil fancies me, bless him,' I say.

'No-o-o-o-o-o-o way!' says Megan in her dramatic way.

Amber – the cheek of her – says sarkily, 'Oh, didn't you know? Half the male population's in love with Danni – apparently. Hold on – what's going on over there?'

A small crowd has gathered outside the Spar. Emily Morgan, who loves a bit of trouble, is clapping her hands together, chanting, 'Fight! Fight! Fight!'

We push through the crowd and Amber does a little gasp of horror. 'It's Neil!' she says.

This is really horrible. In the middle of the circle is Mickey the Thicky, pushing and hitting Neil, his horrible, fat spotty chin jutting out. 'Come on then, Lizard Boy,' he's saying. 'Think you're better than me, do ya?'

Neil looks terrified and has a cut lip. It turns out that he saw Mickey nicking sweets from the Spar and told him to put them back. Thicky, like always, went ballistic. 'You're just a freaky geek boy who plays with lizards,' he's saying, pinning him against the wall. Poor terrified Neil is trying to protect his face with his hands.

Me and Amber look at each other, horrified. Should we wade in? Thicky's about twice the size of us and he would definitely hit girls.

Then we feel someone pushing through the crowd. It's Sean. God, I've never seen him look so angry! 'Lay one more finger on my cousin and you'll regret it, you psycho meat-head,' says Sean.

Thick Mick just laughs. (Sean is also about half his size, to be fair.)

'Come on then, little squirt,' says Thick Mick. 'This'll be funny.'

I look round expecting to see Damian backing his friend up, but he's right at the back of the crowd with Treasure, HOLDING HER COAT!

I don't really see what happens next it's all so fast, but suddenly Mick is flying backwards through the air and Sean is rubbing his fist. Mick gets up again, furious, and punches Sean in the face. He staggers backwards, but then recovers and just runs at Mick bent over in a right angle and headbutts him in the stomach. Thicky falls over, winded and moaning, 'I'm gonna be sick.'

Everyone starts cheering for Sean, who just picks up his coat and says, 'C'mon, Neil.' The crowd disperses and Sean and Neil come face to face with Damian.

'I was just coming to help you, mate,' stutters Damian to Sean.

'No, you weren't!' says Amber, outraged.

'I didn't need any help,' says Sean. 'I just needed to wind him in the right place.'

Neil looks a bit embarrassed, as you would do if your slightly younger cousin had just saved you in front of the entire year.

'Damian doesn't believe in violence. He's a pacifist,' twitters Treasure to no one in particular.

Personally I am prepared to give Damian the benefit of the doubt. It did happen very quickly. Plus he does look totally gorgeous in his black leather jacket.

And anyway, Amber should approve of people being pacifists. Shouldn't she?

8 p.m.

The Spar man has lodged an official complaint with the school. Thicky, Sean and Neil are all in a week's detention and are getting official letters written to their parents. Amber thinks this is a monstrous injustice and that we should boycott lessons until Sean and Neil are let off.

Yeah, right.

Mum comes in and says she's sorry about the clothes thing. Her stomach is getting huge now. She looks like she's been eating too many baked beans and has severe bloating.

Phoebe has shoved a doll cushion up her jumper and shrieks, 'I'm having a baby. Rick is going to be the daddy!' How to tell her that sentence is wrong on SO many levels?

Tuesday

9 a.m.

Amber won't let this Justice for Sean and Neil thing go, or 'JSN' as she calls it. She's as daft as a brush, as Gran would say. At least she's realized that boycotting lessons will get us all excluded. So her parents have suggested – yes, her hippy parents! – that we go on homework strike instead.

Neil thinks it's a brilliant idea, but Sean is mortified. He hates being the centre of attention.

Amber texted about 15 people last night and urged them to text everyone else and get the message out. I kid you not – this is what she wrote:

> Comrades, what happened to Neil Wilson and Sean O'Connor on Monday was an outrage. The teachers were wrong to punish them and we should campaign to get their detention and parental letters cancelled. History teaches us that we must fight injustice. I hope you'll join us.

I know. She's mental.

Lunchtime

Amber is having a meeting in the field behind school re. the JSN thing. I could die for her. She'll be lucky if two people show up.

12.30 p.m.

Amber and Megan trudge round the back field with me about three paces behind. This is going to be so embarrassing. Plus it's starting to drizzle and my hair will go frizzy. 'Amber, I'm giving this mad idea two minutes and then . . .'

Omigod.

There are about THIRTY people here from our year. Including Mickey Taylforth. How thick is this boy?

Amber smiles.

Neil is at the front with Sean, who looks like he wishes he could teleport himself to another planet. Standing next to them are Treasure and Damian. 'You're a star for doing this, Amber,' says Neil, grinning, and giving her a fist bump (ugh – fist bumps are so naff. And he's still got a scab on his lip).

'Yeah, erm, thanks,' says Sean looking like

he'd much rather have the detention than all this fuss.

I smile sympathetically. I'm about to say it's nice but probably won't do any good when Damian steps forward and speaks to Amber. 'Nice one. This is so cool, Amber. I'll back you all the way.'

Quick. I must act quickly.

'Well, it was both our idea really,' I say, stepping forward and putting my arm round Amber. 'We thought it up in my bedroom, last night, didn't we, Amb? Didn't WE?'

Amber rolls her eyes at me but nods at Damian. 'Yes, Danni's VERY enthusiastic about the whole thing.'

Treasure's face is a picture. Wish I had a camera.

Damian must feel guilty for not helping Sean.

Amber gives a speech about injustice and how 'evil flourishes when good men and women do nothing'. It's detention, Amb, not World War Two.

3 p.m.

This thing is gathering momentum. Amber's now got 50 signatures.

The teachers say if we don't do our homework we'll all be in detention. Ha. As if!

4.30 p.m.

Mum's midwife, Wendy, is there when I get home. Rick whispers, 'You wouldn't pick a fight with her on a dark night. Wonder where she left her broomstick?' Quite funny for him. She's got a face like a boxer dog with toothache and talks to Mum like she's five years old.

'And how is Mum feeling? Is Mum tired?' she says in a sing-song voice, as though my mother is drooling in a high chair. 'Will this strapping son and daughter be taking baby out for a walk when he's here so Mum can get some sleep?'

Strapping? Cheeky moo. She can talk.

Weirdly, Simon absolutely HATES her. It's bizarre because normally he loves everyone. He came running in like a missile, sniffed her crotch, then crouched on the floor like a lion, growling at her every time she tried to touch my mum. He had to be locked outside. I can hear him howling. I've just looked out of the window and he is trying to bury his beloved Ugg boots in the garden. Probably to keep them safe from her.

I go into the living room. 'Ah, and this is your second eldest?' asks Witch Wendy.

'Yes, I'm Danni, the ignored beta child,' I say snippily.

She pats Mum's hand. 'Don't worry – the older children always feel threatened when a new baby comes into the nest. It'll pass.'

Nest? What are we – budgies?

The midwife dislikes Simon too. A lot. She says

that a woman of my mum's age (she'll be 45 when the baby comes!) carries enough risks giving birth to a child without having a 'dog's germs' in the house. How ridiculous. Simon has a bath every month with Pears shampoo. When I remember.

She looks at me like I am a pathetic little girl when I say this. 'Any other pets?' she asks, licking her lips like Cruella de Vil.

'No!' I say at the very same second that Mum says, 'Yes.'

'Deirdre doesn't count – she's in a cage,' I say.

'Who's Deirdre? says Witch Wendy, looking puzzled. Mum tells her. 'A rodent? A CAGED rodent?' she's saying. Honestly this woman is hysterical. She's in the wrong job. 'Rodents are filthy,' she says. Well, yes, Deirdre does eat her own poo, sometimes straight from her own bottom. And she smells, and she wees on her own apple chunks, but she's tiny. 'Rodents carry Weil's disease, which could kill a baby,' says Wendy so seriously that her jowls shake.

'Oh dear,' says Mum. 'Perhaps Deirdre better go in the shed?'

Over my dead body.

Thursday

Amber's mum has now helped her set up a Facebook page for the JSN. It's got 500 followers! This morning NO ONE in English handed in their homework, including Thick Mick, but he never does anyway so it doesn't count. Mrs Shutterton looked rattled. She didn't know what to do. It was brilliant!

The headmaster calls Amber to his office and tells her that she's being highly irresponsible. Amber tells him it's 'a moral crusade' and that, with respect, it was irresponsible of teachers to punish the victims as well as the bully. Damian's right – Amber is quite cool.

Friday

No one in our year has handed in homework for biology, history, geography, maths or French. The looks on the teachers' faces are hilarious! I hope we don't resolve this crisis too soon. The teachers hold an emergency meeting.

We are all given letters to take home to our parents warning that we must do our homework. I throw mine in the bin.

Sunday

Thank God for pregnancy hormones. Mum seems to have forgotten all about putting Deirdre in the shed, especially now that I've hidden her cage behind my bin.

Mum's bump seems even bigger. I suppose I should start getting used to the idea. Hope it's a boy. And Phoebe's getting a bit big to ride on Simon's back. Yes, I should be grown-up and welcome this new addition to the family even if it makes my parents FONs – Freaks of Nature

Monday

Fame – for some . . .

The homework boycott is in the local paper!

'Pupils in homework strike', says the headline. 'Kids rap Sir for punishing "innocent" classmates.' Mr Cook asked the photographer not to take pictures of the school, but he did it anyway, and they took quotes from the Facebook site and the letters to our parents. Amber and Neil are described as 'Eco-conscious campaigners'. Sean is 'loyal'. Zilch mention of me. Thanks a lot. I AM one of the organizers, you know. Why can't the Press get anything right?

October

Wednesday

The teachers are so worried they hold an emergency assembly. They don't want any more bad publicity. Mr Cook says he is 'very impressed by our sense of fairness and social responsibility' (he's changed his tune) and that if we all hand in our maths and English he'll overlook the rest of it.

'What about Sean and Neil's detention?' asks Amber, putting her hand up.

Mr Cook looks rattled. 'After reconsidering the matter and speaking to all three parties again, I have decided that the punishment may have been unduly harsh and will repeal it. But only if all outstanding homework is in by the end of the week.'

Everybody is cheering. Even Thick Mick, who still has to do his detentions. Can someone explain to him that he is the villain of this story?

Well, if Damian doesn't fancy me now, he never will.

Friday

Wendy the Witch comes round again to check on Mum and ask her lots more patronizing questions such as, 'You haven't been eating any unpasteurized cheese or uncooked meat, have you?' Oh yeah, Wend, we feast on raw liver here most days.

Rick offers to take Simon for a walk 'to get him

out the way of the wicked hag'. I'm liking Rick more these days.

Wendy tells Mum a story about a pet Jack Russell which tried to pull a newborn baby out of its cot and eat it. I think this woman needs help.

November

Saturday

Amber's mum and dad are letting her have a little party at her house to celebrate the JSN victory. And Damian's coming! Unfortunately, so is Treasure.

Wear my denim miniskirt and red Converse even though they're a bit tight on me. Also my Scarlet Lady nail polish. Amber is a bit giggly as me and Megan help her put the Quavers and Discos into bowls. She's wearing a T-shirt with a picture of a polar bear on it and some strange orange trousers. I say nothing. It's best that way.

The doorbell rings. Amber's mum answers and I hear her saying, 'Ah, so this is the famous Neil and Sean. Hello – and hello, Damian, and, oh, Treasure? What an unusual name.'

There are about ten other people from our year but I don't notice them because my legs are Bendaroos again. Damian looks GORGEOUS, the best I've ever seen him. He's got a denim jacket on that makes his eyes look really blue. Amber nudges me. 'Shut your mouth,' she hisses. 'You're catching wasps.'

9.30 p.m.

So, we're all drinking Cokes and chilling and having a laugh while Neil tells us about how Thicky actually came and apologized to him, when Treasure, who hates not being the centre of attention, butts in with a glint in her eye.

'So, Danni, my mum saw your mum in Tesco,' she says in her bitchy, sing-song voice. 'You never said she was PREGNANT. That's so FUNNY. She's ancient!'

'She is not ancient for your information, Treasure,' I say, my voice wobbling a bit like it always does when she attacks my family. 'Plenty of women have babies in their forties. Look at, erm, Madonna.'

'Ah, yes – Madonna and Mrs Dench – they've got sooooo much in common. Is there actually any more room in your house for anyone else? Or will Baby Clampett be sleeping in the dog basket?'

I feel my fists twitching but I can't say anything in case it comes out wobbly. Treasure is still talking. 'My dad says you lot breed like rabbits.'

Amber pipes up. 'Shut it, Treasure, you're being a bitch.'

Everyone stops talking and stares.

Treasure is outraged. Then she slowly looks Amber up and down. 'I'd rather be a bitch than look like I've been dragged through an Oxfam charity shop,' she says.

Before I realize it I'm lunging forward and am actually pulling Treasure's hair like a five-year-old, screeching, 'Don't you DARE speak to my best friend like that!' Treasure has hold of my arms and pushes me towards the sofa and somehow we tumble on to it in a big heap, shrieking and pulling hair like in a *Tom and Jerry* cartoon.

Amber's mum comes rushing in, demanding to know what's going on. She cannot believe her eyes – says she's very disappointed in us and that the party's now over.

Damian drags Treasure away, and Sean and Neil trail behind them. Neil turns and whispers, 'I don't blame you for hitting her – she's horrible.' Sean just smiles and winks. Ah, that's nice of them.

Amber is mortified. 'You shouldn't have done that, Dan,' she says. 'But – thanks.' And she gives me a hug.

Sunday

Lying in bed wondering if I can face Treasure at school tomorrow. Feel something sharp and purple in my hair. It's one of Treasure's false nails! Ha – that's her mum's 30 quid down the drain.

Hold on – what's all that shouting and screaming outside? Is that Simon barking?

Dad comes running up the stairs wearing his serious face.

'What's the matter, Father dear? Has someone nicked our car? Hope so,' I say.

He ignores this. 'Danni, get down there now,' he says.

Get dressed quickly and run downstairs two at a time. Mum is in the front garden talking to Mr Sharples from down the road. Mr Sharples says the police are on their way.

'Ooh, what's been stolen?' I say.

Mum turns dourly to me. 'Danielle, Mr

Sharples says Simon has bitten his little girl, Suzie. She's at the walk-in centre with her mother.'

This is ridiculous. Simon likes that little kid. She's younger than Phoebe, and even when she pulls his ears he licks her.

'Rubbish,' I say.

Mr Sharples gets quite angry. He says he didn't see it but old Mr Robinson with the fat cat did. Apparently Simon trotted up to Suzie, who was playing in her front garden while her mum just nipped inside to get her a drink. Suzie put her hand through the gate to stroke him and he snapped. Her finger might need stitches.

I feel sick. Simon is barking in the backyard where Mum has tied him up. A police car pulls up. My head is spinning . . .

12 noon

This is the worst day of my life. The police say they'll have to make more inquiries, but if it turns out to be true we might have to have Simon 'destroyed'. That's police-speak for put down.

No. This can't be happening to me.

Go into the yard. Simon does his doggy smile and wags his tail happily. He's got no idea of the trouble he's in. I sit on the ground and stroke his soft ears. I honestly don't think I can cope if he gets put down. I'll have to run away with him before that happens. I bury my face in his furry brown neck and cry like I did when I was four and Rick cut the tail off my favourite toy elephant. He gets that sadistic streak from Dad.

Black Monday

6 a.m.

Simon is back in his kennel, howling. Mum says he's too dangerous to be in the house. I haven't slept a wink.

8 a.m.

I go downstairs and tell Mum and Dad (the FONs) that I'm too distraught to go to school. For once they don't argue. Text Amber with the terrible news. She promises to come round after school.

10 a.m.

The police come round again. Suzie's finger needed two stitches. They say that since Simon didn't actually attack Suzie and may have thought she was feeding him something through the gate, they can't insist we have him put down. I sit down quickly. I think it might be with relief.

Mum sees the police out and I give Simon a big kiss. The Freaks of Nature look at each other. 'We've been thinking,' says Mum. 'We just can't have Simon in the house when the new baby comes, not after this and what happened in Wales.'

'But Simon would NEVER hurt anyone in this family,' I splutter angrily.

Mum looks upset. 'Look, Danni, it's not fair on the baby – or on us – to risk it. He might be jealous of the baby. You read terrible things in the papers. Wendy said we'd never forgive ourselves if something happened. Anyway, the house is too small as it is. Wendy thinks, and we agree, that he should go back to the animal shelter.'

WHAT?

The animal shelter??!! Go to a new home and be someone else's dog?! No, no, no, no, please, God, no.

I hate that evil, scheming witch, Wendy.

4 p.m.

Amber's here. I've been crying all day and seem to have turned into a human snot machine. I tell her everything. She puts her arm around me and says, 'Man, this is so bad.'

8 p.m.

Mum makes sausage sandwiches. I eat one, even though I'm not speaking to her and I'm a vegetarian. This shows how distraught I am.

Tuesday

Am fretting so much over Simon my stomach doesn't even cartwheel when I see Treasure and Damian walking to school holding hands.

Amber says she's been thinking and that I should calm down. She reckons my mum and dad will come round if I just make Simon behave for a while and there are no more disasters. Yes, I'll devise an SOS (Save Our Simon) plan. I'll make him into the best-behaved dog in the world. Feel a bit better.

5 p.m.

Mum tells me that Dad's phoned the animal

shelter. He's going to see them tomorrow. Rick is disgusted with the FONs and says he'll disown them if they get rid of Simon. 'This baby is a pain in the butt!' he says, and goes out, slamming the door and without even eating his tea.

'Yes, and if you send Simon away I swear I'll leave home and then you won't have to worry about not having enough bedrooms,' I say.

The FONs don't seem to be taking this threat very seriously.

I now know how fond Rick is of Simon. He didn't even tell Mum when Simon made tiny teeth holes in his Kings of Leon CD.

8 p.m.

Simon has a death wish. He has stolen and eaten a full box of Celebrations chocolates, which he took from the cupboard by opening it with his greedy fat nose. With the wrappers on. Plus the cardboard box. Now he has been sick all over the living room carpet, which is vomity enough at the best of times.

Dad says, 'The sooner that dog is rehoused, the better.'

I honestly don't feel like I'll ever be happy again.

Wednesday

Can't concentrate all day at school. Wonder what the people at the animal shelter are saying to Dad? Oh no – maybe they've already taken Simon without me knowing. Maybe it was a trick.

3.15 p.m.

Run home so fast that I fall and take the skin off both my knees. Open the gate. Simon is still here! Though he is sitting miserably in his kennel. I fling myself on him and kiss him. He licks the blood off my knees. Am crying with relief and knee-pain as I stagger through the kitchen door. Witch Wendy is here again. Phoebe is sitting on her KNEE – the little traitor.

'Mum told me about the dog attacking a child,' she says, wagging a finger. 'That dog is a menace.'

I'd tell her what a vicious fat hag she is but I can't because there's a lump the size of a cow in my throat.

'Pooh,' says Phoebe, looking up at Wendy. 'Your breath smells.'

Good old Phoebe.

The good news is that the animal shelter is totally full. The bad news is that Dad's going to get in touch with another one 30 miles away.

Friday

Dad has gone to hospital with Mum for another scan on her bump (actually it's more of a hillock now. I don't think she'll be losing this baby weight in a hurry – she's like a Highland cow). They return with another photograph of the baby, which now looks like a porpoise with fingers. Mum is all emotional (again) and says that I looked like that once. No, I did not. I have never looked like a blob.

'Don't pretend that you love me,' I spit at her. 'You can't love me if you'd send MY baby to a dogs' home.'

Could I really run away?

Saturday

Realize I haven't thought about Damian once this week.

Sunday

Dad's been in touch with a shelter in the next town. He's going to see it tomorrow and wants me to go with him so I can 'put my mind at rest'. I tell him I'd rather boil my own eyeballs.

Simon's still sleeping in his kennel. Me, Amber and Megan pool our money and buy him a giant pork pie.

4 p.m.

Gran's here for the Sunday roast. Realize I haven't eaten anything since yesterday.

If I lose weight, will my nose look bigger or smaller?

Poor Simon can't work out why he's been banished to a kennel. How will he cope when he realizes we've abandoned him? New owners won't know exactly where he likes being tickled on his tummy or that he's scared of trousers flapping on washing lines or that he's in love with a pair of Ugg boots. I sit in the yard with him and cry and cry and cry. Mum's looking out of the window. At least she has the decency to look guilt-stricken. Good.

After 30 minutes I wipe my eyes and go inside. Gran, with great sensitivity, asks if we're still 'getting rid of the dog'. I tell her she's the world's most irritating septuagenarian and isn't it time she went in a home?

Gran ignores me and says we should all be 'savouring the peace and quiet before the new baby comes along.'

I shout that there is no peace and quiet around here because she never ever STOPS TALKING! Dad tells me not to be cheeky, but I can tell he agrees. Not that I'm speaking to him.

Monday

8.30 a.m.

Amber says we have to think of a plan to save Simon. Tell her my plan to run away. 'Don't be stupid, Danni,' she says. 'Who do you think you are – George out of the Famous Five?'

No, I bloody well don't. She had horrible short curly hair and terrible taste in clothes.

5 p.m.

Disaster, catastrophe and misery. The dog shelter says it can take Simon. I'm feel as if I'm going to be sick, but first I stare long and hard at Mum and Dad and say, 'I detest the pair of you and I always will.'

'But, Danni, he's bitten two children now,' says Mum. I think she's about to cry.

'Shut your horrible face!' I scream, and run upstairs to the bathroom and slam the door.

I can hear Rick telling them that they're disgusting.

I feel dizzy and panic-stricken. Dad's taking him tomorrow night – 24 hours away.

Mum comes up the stairs and talks to me through the bathroom door. 'Maybe in a couple of years when the baby's older you can get another dog,' she says.

'I don't WANT another dog. I want Simon,' I wail. Then I open the door, look her straight in the eye and say slowly and deliberately, 'But do you know what I'd really like? Another mother.'

Burst out of the bathroom and run downstairs to Simon's kennel. It's raining. Dad is collecting up all his toys and putting them in a bag, even the Ugg boots.

'Simon's going on his holidays!' says Phoebe. This is what they've told her. They truly are evil.

I grab the dog lead and run with Simon down the street. Mum is in the doorway crying and shouting, 'Where are you going?'

'Away from you,' I scream.

Where do I go now? I've no money, no coat and it's raining.

Amber's.

We don't stop running until we get there. Amber sees us through the living-room window looking like two drowned gerbils and ushers us up to her bedroom without her dad seeing.

Tell her through about a million sobs what's

happened. 'Tomorrow, Amb,' I wail. 'They're taking him away from me TOMORROW.'

Amber hugs me. She's gone quiet, which I know means she's thinking. 'Wait here,' she says. 'I'm going to make some phone calls.'

Ten minutes later she's back. 'Right, sorted,' she says.

'Wha?' I blub.

'Sean's going to hide him,' says Amber.

My best friend is a genius.

She phoned Neil, who came up with an idea and phoned Sean. Sean agreed. He has told his dad that my mum's pregnant and can't cope with the dog at the moment so could they help out by having Simon for a while. His dad's fine with it so long as Simon sleeps with Mitzy in their utility room. I can see him whenever I want.

'At least it gives us some time to think of a plan,' says Amber.

I start crying again, but this time with relief. I love Amber.

So Operation Simon is as follows:

I go home tonight so as not to arouse suspicion. Tomorrow morning I get up at 5 a.m. and sneak round to Sean's with Simon. I leave him there, then run home and get back into bed. When I 'wake up' I pretend that Simon's escaped.

Go home, feeling jubilant. Settle Simon in his kennel. Mum and Dad come rushing out. 'Oh, thank God – we were just about to phone the police,' says Mum.

I ignore both of them and stalk off to bed.

Tuesday

3 a.m.

Have set the alarm on my mobile phone, but what if it doesn't go off? Decide to remain awake until the Rescue Mission kicks off at 5 a.m.

4.45 a.m.

Get up and dressed in five seconds. Tiptoe downstairs. One of the stairs creaks and Phoebe stirs in her sleep. Oh no. She could ruin everything. Hold my breath until she's gone back to sleep. It's dark and freezing cold, and Simon is sitting shivering miserably on his blanket. Poor little thing. 'It's OK, Si,' I whisper. 'You're going to see Mitzy.' I open the gate and we run and run and run.

It's a mile to Sean's house. I'm wheezing like a 50-a-day smoker by the time we get there. Sean's waiting, bless him, on the garden wall with Mitzy. The dogs go mad with joy at seeing each other again, sniffing each other's bottoms in a never-ending circle. 'Thank you, thank you,' I say about 20 times.

'S'all right,' says Sean, doing his weird not-looking-you-in-the-eye thing. He shows me where Simon will sleep – a nice warm utility room with blankets on the floor. Feel weepy as I kiss Simon and turn to go. 'Oh, one more thing,' I say – and hand Sean the Ugg boots. Then I run and run back home again, feeling weirdly excited.

6 a.m.

Am lying in bed back in pyjamas, waiting for Dad to get up. His alarm goes off at 6.15 and I know he'll get up, have a noisy wee, go downstairs and open the door to let Simon in. I count backwards in my head – five, four, three, two, one . . .

'Julie. JULIE!' he's shouting up the stairs. 'The dog's gone!'

Suddenly Mum's up and in my room, demanding to know if Simon's in bed with me.

I do a pretty good job of pretending that I've just woken and am panic-stricken that Simon's gone. 'He must have run away,' I shriek. 'It's all your fault . . .'

Mum and Dad are mortified. This is brilliant! Dad says he'll go and look for him. Ha! Loser.

'He'll be back when he's hungry,' says Mum.

Don't bank on it, Mother.

8.30 a.m.

Meet Amber at the bus stop. Tell her everything went to plan. Her eyes are shining. 'Mission accomplished,' she says.

Sean winks at me conspiratorially during maths. We've decided that only the four of us – me, Amber, Sean and Neil – must know our secret. Damian sees him wink and stares at me. Is he jealous?

Ooooh, I think he's jealous. My heart does a flip. Maybe he's going off Treasure!

3.45 p.m.

Damian and Sean are at the bus stop. I think Damian is asking Sean what's going on. Yes, Sean is trying to shrug and look innocent but is a rubbish actor – he just looks guilty. I AM FINALLY GETTING UNDER DAMIAN'S SKIN.

5 p.m.

Mum is grey-faced as she tells me Simon hasn't returned. 'I'm sorry, love,' she says.

I try to look furious, which is hard because my heart is singing. Damian might fancy me. He might fancy ME, not the walking Bratz doll!

Mum tells Phoebe that Simon's already gone 'on his holidays'.

'But I wanted to pack his case and give him my bucket and spaaaaade,' whines Phoebe.

Mum starts crying again. Does this woman ever stop?

6 p.m.

Eat my tea alone in my room, mainly because I'm texting Sean and reliving The Stare moment over and over again.

Sean is in the park with the dogs. 'Simon's having a grrrrrr8time,' he texts.

That's a very lame pun. I wish he wouldn't do that. And I hope he's not having too great a time. He is still MY dog.

Lie on my bed and think about The Stare again.

Wednesday

8 a.m.

Dad says we'd better tell the police that Simon's missing in case he gets picked up. 'I'll do it!' I lie. 'He's my dog. I'll go to the station with Amber after school.'

'I must say you're dealing with this very well,' says Dad suspiciously. 'Is there anything you're not telling us?' Sad that my father has such a distrustful nature.

10.15 a.m.

Sean comes over at break to whisper that Simon was whimpering a bit last night, probably missing me, so he went down and sat with the dogs in the utility room. This boy is saint material.

Damian looks across the yard at us with a weird look on his face again. I can see Treasure frowning and pulling at his arm, asking him what's wrong.

'Careful, Treasure – frowning gives you wrinkles,' I shout sweetly across the yard.

Thursday

4.30 p.m.

Meet Sean in the park to see Simon after school. He's SO happy to see me. Take him and Mitzy a big, juicy bone each and Sean a Plan B CD to say thanks. He goes red when I give it to him.

Simon and Mitzy are like an old married dog couple.

Friday

Number of times Damian stared at me today: three.

Why is sticking a pen in your ear so pleasurable? Once you start you can't stop. Just say no, kids.

Saturday

Mum and Dad make me and Phoebe go with them to Tesco. I punish them by walking really slowly behind them with my hood up.

'Come on, Slack Alice,' says Dad. I know he's feeling guilty about Simon so he is trying to make me laugh. When we are in the clothes section he creeps up behind Mum and puts a big pair of knickers on her head. Phoebe and Mum are shrieking with laughter but I tell him that he needs to grow up. Anyway, I've seen him do it 163 times before.

At the checkout I refuse to help take the stuff out of the trolley even though Mum is looking quite pale. Very pale, actually. She looks like one of those Elizabethans we learned about in history who put white lead on their faces. I so wish she wasn't having this baby/blob.

Suddenly she starts laughing. Dad has secretly filled the trolley with about 20 super-large tubes of Anusol, the stuff that people put on their bottom if they are suffering from piles. It is a joke to embarrass my mother in front of the whole queue. He has done this before too. Why am I being parented by an overgrown Horrid Henry? Mum is saying, 'Oh Dave, you're a case,' and apologizing to the people behind. 'Oh, hello, Mrs Cavendish,' she says. 'How are things, love?'

And I realize to my everlasting shame that it is Treasure and her mother. Treasure smiles sneeringly as my dad gathers up Tesco's entire stock of Anusol to put back on the shelves.

I am seriously thinking of asking to go into foster care.

Sunday

Me and Amber meet Sean, Neil and the dogs in the park. Simon shows how pleased he is to see me by gently humping my leg. We have quite a laugh, eating chips and watching the swans chase the dogs.

Would Damian be jealous if he could see me now, a laughing, carefree, independent woman?

5 p.m.

Walking home I see Rick. He's walking the streets

and whistling for Simon. Am consumed with guilt.

'I can't stand to think of him cold and hungry,' says Rick. I genuinely think he's going to cry. Oh God.

'Can you keep a secret?' I say. 'About Simon.'

'What?' says Rick, staring.

I tell him everything.

'You lying little brat! I've been mental with worry,' he says. Oh dear. Shouldn't have told him.

Then he smiles. 'Nice one though. It was a cool thing to do.'

Praise from Rick! That's as rare as a singing pig.

December

Monday

7 a.m.

Mum not up to make our breakfast. Again. She's rung in sick. Again. She's going to get fired at this rate. Then we'll have even less food in the house.

4 p.m.

Go home. Mum looks nervous. She tells me to sit down. My heart is beating like the clappers.

Oh, and whaddayaknow? It turns out that another child in the next street has been bitten by a dog. But this time they caught the dog – it's a big brown stray the same colour as Simon. Mr Robinson, the fat owner of the fat cat, said this was the one he saw bite Suzie. He didn't have his glasses on and assumed it was Simon! Suzie's dad's been round to apologize and the police have taken the stray to a rescue shelter.

'So Simon wasn't to blame at all,' wails Mum. She's trying to hug me but her big belly's getting in the way. 'I'm so, so sorry. We've let you down. And now we've lost him.'

I walk upstairs, enjoying my moment.

Dad comes home and then trudges sheepishly to my room to apologize too. 'I don't know what to say, Dan,' he says. 'We're a pair of pillocks.'

'Yes, you are,' I say. 'But fortunately I'm a thousand times cleverer than the pair of you put together.'

Dad is gawping at me quizzically. I'm grinning

triumphantly. 'Wait here,' I say, running to get my coat.

5 p.m.

Sean seems sad to let Simon go. 'I've enjoyed having him,' he says a bit sulkily.

'Come and see him any time!' I say. 'Mum will think you're the nicest boy in the world when I tell her what's happened.'

Skip home with my dog. I know Mum's going to offer to take me shopping for clothes too in an attempt to grovel. There is a God.

5.45 p.m.

Mum and Dad are standing in our front garden/ scrapyard waiting as I walk down the street with Simon. Like the lovely, forgiving animal that he is, Simon gallops to lick them and sniff their crotches too.

'Is that . . . ? What? Eh? How?' says Mum, clearly only capable of saying words of one syllable.

'I think we can safely say that our daughter is a conniving, duplicitious, disobedient little HORROR,' says Dad. Then he bends to kiss me on the head. 'That's my girl.'

I tell them what happened, about Amber and Sean and me getting up at 5 a.m. (That'll be the first and last time in your life, says Dad sarkily.) Phoebe wants to know if Simon's brought her a present back from his holidays. Mum says, 'Well, Sean sounds a nice boy. You must bring him round for tea.' See – what did I say?

Tuesday

It is all around school about the SOS project. At break people gather round the four of us asking if it's true that Sean and Neil hid Simon for a week in a secret attic and he lived on dead mice. Yes, we lie, because it sounds more exotic than the truth. Damian is standing so close to me I can smell his hair gel. I have turned the colour of a lobster. My cheeks are so hot I think they might be hissing.

Treasure hates all the fuss over me. 'It's only a DOG,' she says. 'The disgusting dog, might I add, whose poo Danni sprayed all over Damian. Ugh, they shouldn't be allowed near people.'

I'm thinking up one of my more cutting replies when I realize Damian's speaking. 'Treasure?' he says. 'Why don't you just shut up for once?'

I think I might have died and gone to heaven.

6 p.m.

I'm in my bedroom with Amber and Megan eating chocolate buttons. 'So what do you reckon?' I'm saying to them. 'Do you think this is my moment with Damian? Did you see him looking at me? He was looking at me, wasn't he? Do you think he admires me or fancies me? Or admires AND fancies me? Should I buy some new clothes and move in for the kill?'

Amber has gone a bit quiet and Megan's saying half-heartedly, while eyeing Deirdre's cage warily, 'Yeah, sure – if that's what you want.'

What I want? They KNOW it's all I've thought about for a year.

'Amber?' I say.

'Mmm, well – it's, er, just that I think you can do a lot better than Damian,' she says.

Better than Damian? Ha hahahahaha! With whom – JLS?

'Look, I'm just saying there's plenty more fish in the sea. Look around you. Open your eyes.'

'Yes, Amber,' I say. 'And when I open my eyes I see a vision of gorgeousness and, lo, it is Damian.'

'He's not all THAT handsome,' she says.

Memo to Amber: you definitely should have gone to Specsavers.

8 p.m.

In kitchen with Mum. 'Wendy came round again today,' she says. 'She's spitting feathers that we're keeping Simon. Strange woman. Oooh, there's a hardness to her.'

Hardness? She'd make Fu Manchu look like Makka Pakka.

Wednesday

Call into the sweetshop on the way home from school for some Mega Dust sherbet. Am tipping it down my throat when Mrs Papadopoulos who lives opposite comes running up. 'Valerie . . .' she says (she has always, for some reason, thought my name was Valerie), 'Valerie, there's an ambulance outside your house. I hope everything's all right.'

Why do people say this? Do people usually call ambulances when everything is all right?

My stomach feels like it has dropped into

my legs. Run home imagining a life without a mother when I see her being carried out on a sort of stretcher on wheels by two paramedics. I must say she looks awful. 'Mum, what is it? What's UP?'

The paramedics say that she was found collapsed at home. She had been trying to light the flame-effect gas fire in the living room when she keeled over and fainted. Her hair and eyebrows are all singed, but she's telling me not to worry.

'Mother,' I say, 'you look like something out of *Tom and Jerry*. Seriously, you don't want to look in a mirror.'

Mr Ainsworth from next door appears. 'I called the ambulance,' he said. 'It was that dog of yours.'

Oh God above – what's Simon done now?

Dad emerges carrying Phoebe and looking dazed. 'That dog is a total and utter . . .' I screw my face up in pain like I've just stubbed my toe, '. . . SUPERSTAR,' he declares, getting into the ambulance. 'He was with your mum when she fainted. He jumped over the wall into the Ainsworths' garden and wouldn't stop barking until they followed him back into the house. God knows what could have happened if he hadn't been there.'

There are a million things I could say here. But this is not a time for smug told-you-so's.

I climb into the ambulance. Sod it. 'I told you so,' I say smugly.

I think I'll rename him Saint Simon.

6 p.m.

It turns out that Mum is severely anaemic, which is quite common in pregnancy, and that's what's been making her so tired and pale. The baby takes all your body's iron, the doctor said, and it makes you faint. So babies are basically just thieves.

The good news is that Witch Wendy should have been monitoring this for weeks but she has clearly been too busy obsessing over my dog instead. Apparently she'll get into trouble for this. Yippee.

The doctor gives Mum massive iron tablets. 'These might cause constipation and piles,' he says.

I remember the Anusol in Tesco and for what feels like the first time in days, I laugh.

Mum is changing midwives.

She's also found out that she's having . . . a boy. I hope his feet don't stink like Rick's.

Thursday

Dad buys Simon two steak-and-kidney pies.

Friday

Mum says Simon can have the Ugg boots forever. 'Aaaaaaah,' says Phoebe, clutching her hands to her chest. 'Now they can get married!'

Saturday

This is unbelievable.

Rick has just come back from taking Simon for a walk – and guess what? When he was at the Memorial Gardens there was another boy there, aged about 18, who Simon kept running up to, then running away, then running back up to him and running away, like he does when he's found a dead bird. The boy seemed confused until he suddenly said, 'That dog's not Shrek, is it?'

Rick was about to say, 'No – Shrek is a cartoon ogre and this is a mongrel dog, you great numpty,' but then the boy said, 'It is, it is!'

Oh my God – it turns out that this boy, Aidan, used to be Simon's owner before we got him from the shelter! Except that they called him Shrek.

But this isn't the best of it. Oh no. Aidan's mum

is . . . big drum roll . . . Witch Wendy! She is like the serpent, that woman.

It was her that wanted rid of the dog, not Aidan, and she kept 'forgetting' to buy Shrek food. One day Aidan came home from school and she said Shrek had ripped up her best cushion (quite possibly true, given his past form) and that she'd taken him to the rescue shelter. Except really she'd just tied him up outside Asda thinking that someone else would do it.

Rick told Aidan what had happened and he was furious but said his mum has always been weird. Weird? She needs to be put in a padded cell.

I don't think she realized Simon used to be her dog when she came to our house. He's a lot fatter for a start. She just hates all dogs. But Simon knew her, which is why he growled at her . . .

This feels like the end of an episode of *Scooby-Doo*.

Sunday

Neil is letting me copy his maths homework. I go round to his to collect it. Sean is there. I tell him about the Simon/Aidan/Witch Wendy triangle. Sean says he's going to find out where she lives and let Mitzy do a poo on her front step.

Wish I'd thought of that.

Monday

Teacher gives me a pep talk about my 'attitude' after I get a C plus in French. 'You're so quick-witted, Danni,' she says. 'I just wish you'd use it for your schoolwork instead of making smart-arse remarks all the time.'

Aaaaaaaaaaaaaaaaaah. A teacher said 'arse'. I'm going to tell.

Tuesday

Damian keeps looking at me again. You know when you just know that someone's staring and you can feel the side of your head prickling but when you look at them they look away and start scratching their nose? Like that. He did that four times in biology. Of course he could be staring at the pus-filled spot on my forehead which is the size of Phoebe's space hopper and which I've tried to cover up with my fringe.

He's still wearing her stupid bracelet. Damn. My Damian obsession is returning to max.

What am I going to wear for the school Christmas Disco? That's what I'd like to know. There is only a week to go. My mother SO owes me.

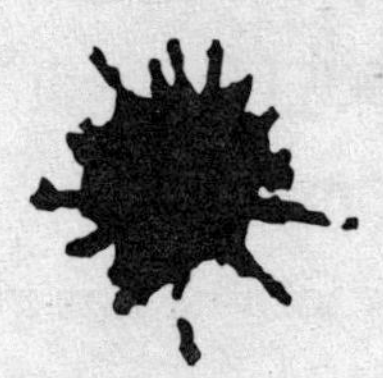

Wednesday

7 p.m.

Quelle result. Mum and Dad gave me £20 because of all I've been through, and Gran gave me £10, although she said I wasn't to tell Rick or Phoebe because on her pension she can't be giving out tenners willy-nilly and it's shocking what old people have to live on in this day and age and have I seen the price of gas, until I passed out with boredom on the sofa.

Saturday

Operation minidress. I'm in town with Amber. Mission: to buy a minidress that will blow Treasure Cavendish out of the water. Have found the perfect one on the internet. It's made of pale blue lace, which I feel will bring out the colour of my eyes and make Damian gaze into them and realize what a fool he has been.

Get to shop. There's only one left. It's a size too small but I'm determined to get into it anyway.

'It's too small,' says Amber, sitting on the floor of the changing room. 'The seams are straining across your bum.'

Does she want to live to see her next birthday?

Question: Can you go down a dress size in three days? Course you can.

I buy the dress.

I will eat only yoghurt between now and Tuesday.

7 p.m.

I'm starving and everyone's watching *The X Factor* and eating fish and chips, including Gran, who keeps saying how delicious they are. I make a play of not wanting any because I'm on a diet, then rush into the kitchen and steal chips off Phoebe's plate when she's not looking.

8 p.m.

I am starving. Now I know how Kate Moss feels.

Sunday

Still starving. Cannot resist a fried-egg sandwich for breakfast. Gran says, 'Fried food will make that huge spot on your head even bigger. And it will play havoc with your packet.'

What's the jail sentence for murdering your gran?

Tuesday

Day of the School Christmas Disco

8 a.m.

Poo, poo and triple poo. Gran was right. The spot on my forehead has had babies. My tete is now an acne community centre.

Also I have lost . . . no weight.

Mum, who's still being nice, says I can borrow some of her Benefit concealer tonight. Thank God.

9.30 a.m.

Treasure comes over before geography. She's actually smiling at me! 'Are all of you coming to the disco tonight?' she asks, super-friendly.

'All who?' I say.

'You and the 27 boils on your head,' she says. All her nasty Klingons erupt into laughter.

'Well, at least my head's full of something other than fresh air – airhead,' I reply. It's a lame riposte, but she's hurt me and it's the best I can think of.

Then she leans forward and hisses, 'Stay away from Damian, Clampett.'

'Why should I,' I say?

'Because one, he's way out of your league. and two—'

'Ooh, ooh!' I say. 'Give the girl a sticker. Treasure can count to two!'

Oh yes. I think that shut her up.

6 p.m.

This is going to be hell. I am going head to head with Treasure for Damian and she'll have a new outfit and look like a supermodel, whereas my skin is like pink semolina pudding. But I am ready for my fate. Weirdly I feel quite relaxed, as if I've taken a chill pill. I am wearing:

1. My lace minidress, £29.99
2. My 1960s beret, which my mum says makes me look like Twiggy – whoever he is.
3. Some tinsel around my neck. It's ironic – OK?

I look pretty good, despite the skin and the fact this dress is so tight I can hardly speak.

The doorbell goes. Megan is here! She is

wearing . . . eugh, a prom-type dress in pink and white silk. Does she realize we are not extras in *Grease, the Musical*?

'You look like a giant trifle,' says my dad as I kick him under the table. He is SO rude. Megan looks a bit chinned until my father hastily adds, 'I meant that you look scrumptious.'

'You look, er, amazing,' I wheeze in my tight dress.

'Are you OK?' says Megan. 'Your face looks a bit purple.'

The doorbell rings again. Amber is here! She is wearing . . .

. . . erm, green cords. Again.

But she looks quite pretty, with her hair tied up and a red top on instead of the usual dreary black boys' T-shirt. 'I'm probably only staying an hour,' she says. Sigh.

Amber tells me I must promise not to cry tonight, whatever happens. As if.

7 p.m.

Dad drops us off at school. 'Be good – and if you can't be good, be careful,' he says, for the four-millionth time in his life. I don't say anything because I can't seem to breathe.

'That dress is going to split if you're not careful,' says Amber, ever the ray of sunshine.

Biggins Bad Breath is minding the door. Wearing trainers. I'll say it again – he's wearing TRAINERS. Teachers should not be allowed to wear normal people's clothes. It makes them look like they're one item short of a meal deal.

Oh, look. They've put balloons and a big inflatable Father Christmas in a net hanging from the ceiling. Hello? Do they think we are all still wearing pull-up pants? Still, at least there's a DJ and the music is loud, loud, loud . . . We walk in all casual, but my head is swivelling, scanning the room like a meerkat for D and T. They aren't here yet.

I swing my hair a bit.

'You look nice,' says Sean, suddenly apparating like Harry Potter.

WHAT did he say? I look nice? Does he even notice such things? 'Thanks, so do you,' I say, because my mum says that you should always return a compliment. Actually he does look quite nice in a boring white-T-shirt-and-jeans way, not like a big square in the short sleeved pale blue shirt he usually wears for school.

The girls and me ask for three Dr Peppers from the bar. 'Bad Romance' comes on so we go and dance. One of the boys is doing quite funny Lady Gaga impressions on the dance floor. This is quite a laugh. No, it isn't. Treasure and Damian have just walked in and she looks A.M.A.Z.I.N.G. Every head in the room turns to look at her like they do on films. She has had her hair put in rollers and blow dried so it's mega curly, and she is dressed in a red dress, red hairband, red cardigan and red sparkly shoes. I don't hate her.

I loathe and despise her. Damian looks his usual miserable self.

'Hi, Danni' says Treasure. 'Brave of you to come – and in one of your little sister's dresses. You look like 10 pounds of potatoes in a 5-pound sack.'

Yes, I definitely loathe her.

8.30 p.m.

Some boy from Year 10 is doing the DJ-ing and a load of girls from our year are hovering round him like giggly flies. He's playing 'I Just Can't Get You Out of My Head' by Kylie. This is a bit retro, but at least it's not a. . . oh no. Now it's George Michael's 'Last Christmas' – a slowie. Just what I was dreading.

Treasure has her head resting on Damian's shoulder like a big, wet limpet, but her eyes are open and scanning the room like a basilisk to make sure I'm watching.

Damian, I'm delighted to say, looks as stiff as a Topshop dummy. Where is Amber when you need her? Oh, look, she's sitting with Neil, probably discussing how to save the two-headed natterjack or something. She looks over and gives me a shrug which says, It's crap that they are slow dancing in front of your very eyes – but, hey, what can you do?

Smack Treasure over the head for starters.

I go and pull Amber out of her seat. 'Let's go and play pool in the other room with some of the lads,' I say with a frozen smile on my face. I must be breezy. I MUST BE BREEZY.

Amber looks a bit grumpy. Hello? I thought best friends were supposed to be supportive.

Someone touches my shoulder. It's Sean again. For some reason he is holding a balloon, which makes him look a bit, you know, simple. 'I know you're feeling sad, but it's really not worth worrying about,' he says.

Oh yeah? Try living in my brain for a week.

Sean is still talking. 'I've told Damian I don't know how he can spend so much time with Treasure. She's so boring – and thick.'

What? I'm liking this – tell me more. He then does quite a funny impression of Biggins Bad Breath, who is always saying, 'An hour in detention is an hour of your life that you will NEVER. EVER. GET. BACK,' except that Sean says, 'An hour listening to Treasure talk about the latest top that her mother brought her back from her latest mini-break to Paris is an hour that you will spend in a DEEP, DEEP COMA, possibly never regaining consciousness.'

I snigger. A lot. 'Oh, don't worry about me. I'm fine,' I say. And I am actually. Weirdly.

9 p.m.

Megan comes running over in her *Grease* prom dress looking like a shiny meringue. She is so excited her ears have gone bright pink. 'Guess what,' she says. 'Eliza Bowman saw Damian and Treasure when they were first walking in and they were bickering.

'Apparently,' she goes on, breathing quite deeply so that she sounds like she's giving birth (she loves reporting gossip), 'Damian feels that he doesn't see enough of his mates any more.'

Really? REALLY? Oh, thank you, thank you, thank you. Didn't I always say there was a God? But deep down I don't feel as thrilled by this news as I thought I would. Strange. And anyway, they're both still wearing each other's pathetic bracelets. And she's still draped over him like a cheap rug. They're not exactly OVER, are they?

9.10 p.m.

I need to have a quiet think. Plus this dress is killing me. Oh, how nice. The girls' toilets are out of order because someone has tried to flush a sanitary towel and blocked one toilet and the other one hasn't worked for about four years anyway. Bad Breath Biggins is now policing the doorway of the boys' toilets so that we all can use them but not boys and girls at the same time.

'You can't go in at the moment,' he says, like he's guarding the Crown Jewels. 'Andrew Slater's in there.'

'Oh well, we'll be here all night then,' I say. 'By the time he's finished checking his reflection in the mirror.' (He's quite vain.) BBB looks like he's actually smirking at that but he says nothing.

Andrew comes out smoothing his hair so I go in and as I do there's a simpering voice behind me. 'Please, Mr Biggins, sir, can I go in with Danielle. I'm bursting.'

It's Treasure. Why does this always have to happen to me?

'Yes, yes, but hurry up,' says Biggins. He's now another person I would like to put on my fantasy shipwreck. (This is a collection of people I don't like who I would like to be marooned together forever on a desert island with only broccoli to eat.)

I sit down for a wee in one cubicle while Treasure sits down in the other. 'How's your poor mum?' I hear her say in her faux concerned voice through the partition wall.

'Fine – why shouldn't she be?' I say, pulling some toilet roll out of the dispenser really hard.

'It's just that Dad heard about her collapsing the other day. He says it must be so hard at her age.'

I can feel my blood boiling like a kettle but luckily I am distracted by some small commotion I can hear outside in the disco room. Maybe they've let down all those balloons from the ceiling. How will we ever contain our excitement? 'Actually it was nothing to do with her age,' I say coolly. 'Anaemia can happen in pregnancy even if you're 18.'

'Well, look on the bright side,' says Treasure.

'After the baby's born she can sterilize her teeth at the same time that she's sterilizing the baby's bottles.'

I have to admit that's quite a good line by her standards. But I'm so angry I bang the partition wall like a madwoman. 'Why are you so totally, totally VILE, Treasure?' I scream.

'Me?' she splutters. 'You're the vile one, always trying to steal my boyfriend. You must know he's not interested by now. He says your family are all weird but I think he's being kind. I think the phrase he's looking for is "unhygienic Clampett freaks".'

Time seems to stand still. I think about my lovely little sister being called a freak. I think about the way she collects slugs in the garden and gives them individual names and apartments made of pebbles and I feel this rage coming over me like the Incredible Hulk, which is apt really because my dress is about to split.

I clamber to stand up on the toilet seat so that I can see over the partition. Treasure looks a bit worried to be honest, as she sits there with her knickers round her ankles looking up at me while I jab my finger at her from above.

'Don't you DARE call my family freaks,' I say, tottering on the seat a little. 'At least we don't spend all our time shopping and simpering and being thick and walking round with skin the colour of a Satsuma – aaaaarrrrgh!'

Oh no. Somebody shoot me.

We are not alone. I turn my head and see that – oh dear lord, no – Damian, Sean and Nerdy Neil are standing there with their mouths wide open. They heard everything. I slip and feel a wet sensation on my leg. One of my feet has gone down the toilet . . .

'What are you doing in here?!' I splutter, trying to hide the fact that I have a dripping, pee-stained shoe. 'This is girl-weeing time. Biggins is supposed to be guarding the door.'

Damian's face is blank.

Oh well, he certainly won't fancy me now. Sean says that a couple of lads got into a fight on the dance floor and Biggins had to go and sort it out. 'We were worried about you. You've been ages,' he says awkwardly, looking at his shoes again. 'Amber is searching for you everywhere.'

Damian says absolutely nothing.

Treasure has now pulled up her knickers, opened her cubicle door and is rushing into Damian's arms. 'Take me home,' she says with these little fake sobs. 'I think I'm going to faint. She's been HORRIBLE to me. And it's all because she wants you for herself. I've told her that you think she's a freak.'

Drama queen – much? That girl should win an Oscar. Damian looks at her with a strange expression on his face, but steers her out of the door.

'You didn't wash your hands!' I shout feebly after her.

Sean puts a hand on my arm. 'We heard what she said about your family and the, er, sterilized teeth,' he says. 'Oh, and obviously the bit about you trying to steal her boyfriend.'

My cheeks burn at the thought of Damian knowing that I have been plotting for so long.

Someone's coming back into the toilets. What is this – a coffee morning?

It's Damian – alone. 'Danni, I, er, just wanted to say that Treasure was out of order then. I did say you were a bit of a freak after, you know, the thing in the park, and after that time when I came round and you were sitting on top of the dog painting its face. But I don't think that now. In fact, I think you're great. Better than great. I think you're cool. I'll ring you.'

I'm standing there staring into his handsome face. And I can think only one thing: he is actually wearing CONCEALER!

I watch his back as he walks out of the door.

'Let's go and find Amber and get out of here,' I

say to Sean and Nerdy Neil. 'But first can you tell me something?'

'What?' they say together.

'Why do boys' toilets smell so bad?'

9.30 p.m.

We're all walking home – me with a squelchy shoe, Sean, Amber and Neil. Amber and Neil are talking about something boring, and me and Sean are walking slightly behind – in silence. Suddenly he coughs and says, 'For what it's worth, you know, I think you're way prettier than Treasure. I always did. Damian thought I was mad to think that.'

Gee – thanks.

Still, Sean thinks I AM WAY PRETTIER THAN TREASURE!!

'Do you? DO YOU?' I say. 'In exactly what way "prettier"?' (Yes, I am fishing for compliments, but I so rarely get my ego boosted.)

'I just think you're lovely. A couple of times I was mad with you for saying mean things to Neil, but I know why you do it, I think. It's when you're nervous. And I've must say – you can be really funny.'

Sean O'Connor thinks I'm lovely and funny! Sean O'Connor thinks I AM LOVELY AND FUNNY. How strange is this night turning out to be?

'And you've got what you want now,' he says in a small voice. 'Damian told me the other day that's he's fancied you for a while.'

Wake me up, I'm dreaming. 'Why didn't you tell me?' I say.

He goes quiet. 'Because I was jealous,' he says eventually.

And then I realize how weird life is. Because someone is saying the words 'I'm not interested in Damian any more', and I realize that person is me. What's more, I mean it. I really mean it. I think of how he never helped Sean in his fight with Thick

Mick and how he never once told Treasure to shut up when she was being cruel to people and, worse, how he was wearing concealer on his spots. And how he's actually quite DULL.

And now I'm thinking about Sean, remembering all the times this term when he'd smile at me in French and how if it wasn't for him Simon might be back in the animal shelter and how brave he was standing up for Neil.

'But I thought all boys fancied Treasure,' I say. 'I mean – look at her tonight. She's gorgeous. And those red sparkly shoes!'

Sean looks at me as if I'm mad. 'Are you completely demented?' he says. 'Danni, she looked like a Barbie Dorothy from *The Wizard of Oz*.' A snort comes down my nose and then I'm doing big, proper belly laughs. We walk into the night laughing and laughing and laughing.

Then Sean says, 'Er, Danni – I should tell you something. Your dress has split.'

Saturday

10 a.m.

Well, considering that I was humiliated, virtually called a nasty scheming bitch in front of Damian and had a row while standing on a boys' stinky toilet seat, which the whole school now knows about, I think last night went quite well.

Sean is the nicest boy I have ever met. I can't believe I couldn't see how much cooler and funnier and more interesting he is than Damian. It's me that needs my eyes tested.

12 noon

Mum is making bacon sandwiches. Her tummy's so big now she can hardly turn round in the kitchen. Dad is fussing around her like an old woman, saying, 'You need to conserve your energy for the birth, pet.'

Mum looks at him witheringly. 'No, what I will need for the birth, Dave, is lots of painkilling drugs. Now shut up and eat your sandwich. But we've run out of brown sauce.'

Typical.

Because I am a strict vegetarian I only have one rasher of bacon on mine.

2 p.m.

Amber calls round. About time. I've been texting her all morning. Where has she been? You just can't rely on some people.

'I told you about a million times,' she says. 'I've been to that protest against the plans to chop down six trees to build a new leisure centre near the park.'

'Oh yeah, I vaguely remember you saying something about that,' I say. 'Anyway, let's talk about me.'

Amber rolls her eyes. 'I saw Neil at the protest,'

she says. 'He bumped into Damian this morning. He and Treasure had a huge argument on the way home. He's not sure if he wants to go out with her any more. Apparently she's been in tears ever since.'

Hmm, I feel less smug about the thought of Treasure crying than I thought I would.

'It was a good night in a funny way, wasn't it?' I say.

Amber's face brightens. 'It was great!' she says. 'Me and Neil—'

'You'll never guess what Sean said to me,' I interrupt, lying back on my bed with my hands behind my head. I know it's rude to butt in, but I don't want her getting carried away droning on about some eco-issue again. She doesn't know when to stop.

She sighs. 'He said he really likes you and always has.' Amber has adopted a slightly bored voice, I notice.

'Oh thanks. Well, that's ruined my big moment. How did you know?'

'Neil told me.'

'You seem to be doing a lot of cosy talking to Neil these days,' I snap.

'Well, I've been trying to tell you that too, but you've been so, erm, preoccupied with Damian and Treasure lately,' she says awkwardly, fiddling with her 'Don't Be Mean – Go Green!' badge. 'I sometimes wonder if you listen to a word I say that isn't about you.'

'What? How dare you! I do NOT always talk about myself.'

'Then how come you don't know how close me and Neil are then?' says Amber with her hands on her hips. 'Because I could never get a word in.'

Suddenly a clunking great penny drops in my (spotty) head.

'By "preoccupied" you mean 'self-obsessed and selfish', don't you?' I say, slowly feeling the need to chew my fists with shame. Someone shoot me now – I haven't asked Amber a single question about her life for weeks. It's all been about me, me, me. My crush on Damian, my problems with Simon, my shame over my mum's pregnancy, my lack of a tan.

'Maybe Bad Breath Biggins was right after all,' I say. 'Me and Treasure don't spoil a pair. I'm so, so sorry, Amber. After all you've done for me and Simon too. I don't deserve to live,' I wail.

'Oh, don't be so totally melodramatic – again,' says Amber, feeding Deirdre some celery through the bars of her cage. 'You've just had a bit of an, erm, one-track mind lately.'

Yeah, the one track being me and my stupid life.

Amber is still talking. I must concentrate. 'It's just that me and Neil have been texting loads lately and I really, REALLY like him.' Her face is glowing. Even her freckles are glowing. She looks really pretty.

'We are going to protest outside the supermarket next Saturday against the use of too much plastic packaging!'

Normally, of course, I'd say, 'Whoopidoo. Can't

wait to ink that special treat into my diary,' but for once I hold the sarcasm. Instead I suggest that all four of us plus the two dogs go for another walk again soon, in the park, by way of a gift from me to her. Amber looks like she might burst with happiness. Honestly, some people are so easily pleased.

'That would be brilliant,' she says, clapping her hands together. I'm so lucky that Amber is my best friend.

I get a text from Damian asking if I'd like to go to the cinema some time. I text back saying I don't think it would be a good idea at the moment as it wouldn't be fair on Treasure. I am SO thoughtful and mature.

Sunday
10 a.m.

I phone Sean. He is so taken aback that I actually dialled his mobile number I worry he is going to faint. 'I've got something to ask you,' I say.

'What?' he says nervously, obviously thinking that I've had second thoughts about Damian.

'Do you want to come for a walk this afternoon with me and Amber. Bring Neil? About 3 o'clock? With the dogs, obviously.'

He laughs in a relieved, sweet sort of way and says, 'That would be wicked.'

Aah. I can't believe such a nice person is interested in a horrible egomaniac like me. Or that anybody still says 'wicked'.

12 noon

Dad shouts up that a friend's at the door to see me. Holy moly! I know Amber's excited about the park, but she's three hours early. I am wearing an old stained dressing gown and have put some of Mum's mud face pack on, which I stole from the bathroom. Safe to say I am not looking my best. Oh well.

I hear feet coming up the stairs so I shout in Miss Judd's robotic, nasally voice, 'Warning, pupils, this bedroom stinks like a zoo. Only enter if you have a peg for your nose. Repeat – A. Peg. For. Your. Nose.'

Deirdre, you see, has just weed all over my chemistry homework, which is quite appropriate given that rodent urine contains large quantities of nitrogen, phosphates and potassium.

The door swings open. I have my back to it. 'Enter!' I say. 'And I promise not to mention tedious, trite, tarty Treasure once,' I say.

'What does trite mean?' says a voice that is definitely not Amber's.

Standing there with Deirdre scurrying over her brand-new Timberland boots is Treasure.

'What? You? Why? Oh!' I say, opening and closing my mouth like a goldfish and, like my mother, only able to say words of one syllable. My enemy is actually standing in my bedroom and I am not equipped for battle, considering that my face is covered in brown sludge, I have a tatty dressing gown on with Marmite stains down the front and Deirdre has peed everywhere. This confirms everything Treasure has ever said about me. I am indeed a Clampett.

Then I see that her eyes and nose are red from crying and she hasn't even bothered to put any mascara on. Holy moly, things must be bad. 'You look terrible,' I say, which is meant to be funny coming from me, but, as usual, this goes over her (air)head.

'Before you start, I have come to apologize,' she says, blowing gallons of snot noisily into a tissue.

'For what?'

'For what I said in the toilets. Damian said it was nasty. And I suppose he's right.'

Hello – am I in a parallel universe? Treasure Cavendish is standing in my house. Asking forgiveness. From moi?

'Which bit are you saying sorry for exactly?' I say, narrowing my eyes.

She lowers her voice. 'You know, about your family being the Clampetts and your mum being old and the house being, er, filthy.' She looks around my cesspit of a bedroom as she says the last bit.

I pick off some of the clay that's drying on my face. 'You shouldn't say stuff about people's families when they've never done anything to you,' I say. 'I never slag yours off.' I take a deep breath and carry on. 'But in all honesty one thing you said was true. I did want Damian for myself. But I don't any more. Cross my heart and hope to wear bifocals.'

She is blowing her nose again and staring in horror at Deirdre, who has chosen this moment to do her party trick of eating her own poo straight from her bottom.

'I know. You're all pally with Sean now, aren't you? Damian says he talks about you a lot. I think he's smitten. Er, should that gerbil be doing that?'

'She's not a gerbil,' I say loftily. 'She's a degu.'

Treasure is now sitting tentatively down on my Ikea duvet cover which, naturally, is covered in Simon's dog hairs. She quickly stands up again.

'This coat cost a hundred quid,' she says.

She looks so miserable I feel a flicker of pity for her. Only a flicker though. Let's not get carried away or forget how mean she was about my mum. 'Look, I should probably say sorry too,' I say grudgingly. 'I said some vile things to you too. It's only because I was sort of a little bit, well you know, erm, jealous.'

'Oh, I know THAT,' she says. 'And it's totally understandable. I get all these great clothes, and I know I usually look pretty amazing and everyone wants to hang out with me.'

Hello? What kind of person apologizes for their shocking awfulness while reminding you how beautiful they are?

'And you have such rubbish clothes, and my mum says you never go on proper, foreign holidays. And I feel sorry for you having such lank hair and bad acne when I've been so blessed with great skin and can afford to get highlights. But you are quite popular. I'd love people to be my friends DESPITE what I look like, not because of it.'

Can you believe I'm having to listen to this in my own bedroom? What's that horrid whining noise? Oh, it's Treasure. She still seems to be talking.

'Because the thing is, when people tell you you're beautiful, Danni, you feel under pressure to ALWAYS look beautiful. It's exhausting. Sometimes I spend a whole week worrying about what to wear for a party because I know people expect me to look sensational. I've set myself a very high bar. I know it's hard for you to understand but, believe me, good looks can be a curse, Danni. You don't know how lucky you are.'

Oh charming. So, to recap, Treasure has complimented me while managing to deliver three brand-new insults. And I thought my hair was one of my better features . . .

Treasure says she'd better be going because her mum and dad are taking her out for Sunday lunch at Pod, the brand-new restaurant in town, which has computers on every table. Trust her to be the first in our year to go there. I ask what's happening with her and Damian. She looks blubby again. 'He said he wants to cool it off for a while and see more of his friends, but we'll still be mates.' She shows her naked wrist. 'We've taken off our commitment bracelets,' she says, blowing her nose copiously again. 'He wanted me to say sorry. So I have.'

She looks so miserable (and quite ugly! Hooray – Treasure is an ugly crier!) that I decide I can't be bothered to say anything snitty back.

'Look, it was nice of you to come,' I say, 'and I suppose it was quite brave, considering I could have set Deirdre on you. Shall we try to be nicer to each other next term?'

How grown-up am I? How ~~magnamonous~~, ~~manganminous~~ nice am I, eh???

For a minute I think she is going to kiss me, but she's actually leaning over and peering at my neck. Then she says, 'I think you're having an allergic reaction to that face pack.'

2 p.m.

Treasure has gone and I am looking in the mirror contemplating the red, blotchy, peeling horror show that is my visage. Mum says I should only have left it on 10 minutes, but it was more like two hours. I look like the Ood monster out of *Doctor Who* only less attractive. And I'll be in a public park – in daylight! – with Sean within one hour.

Thing is, I don't think he'll mind.

And, on the bright side, I might have embarrassing parents who snog in front of my friends and do not know the meaning of contraception even though they're old-age pensioners, my mother may fail to feed us properly and the towels in the bathroom may always smell of my dad's armpits, but I wouldn't swap my family, actually, if you must know (I'm not even totally hating the idea of meeting the blob now). And Treasure Cavendish – the most fancied girl in our year – has just apologized to ME. My work here is done.

I realize I am humming as I get ready to meet Amber and Sean and Neil and Mitzy with a face like the top of a pizza rustica. Yes, in the words of Kylie Minogue, I know that I am lucky: lucky, lucky, lucky.

2.50 p.m.

Mobile is ringing. Go away. Oh, it's Dad. He's taking Mum to hospital because she's having contractions. God spare us. Is it going to be like that video they showed us in biology about childbirth?

That poor woman was mooing and grunting – she was like an entire FARMYARD, with boobs like big veiny beach balls.

'Your gran's here with Phoebe, and Rick's gone out,' says Dad, all breathless. 'I'll ring as soon as there's any news.'

'OK,' I say, feeling a fluttery sensation in my stomach. The Blob is on its way.

'One more thing, Danni. Mum says since we've given you a hard time recently you can choose your new brother's name. Have a think.'

Oooh, Father, my cup runneth over. How will I ever come down from the excitement of naming the new Dench rugrat?

Hold on though – there is potential to really wind my parents up here. Yes, imagine my dad's face when he has to tell his mates that his new son is called Tarquin Jonquil Tristram Dench.

I walk through the park gates smiling with Simon trotting at my heels . . .

No, I know what I'll call my new baby brother. Yes, yes – it's the obvious choice.

. . . Damian . . .

Hahahaha. KIDDING. I so had you there.

But there is one name I'm more and more liking the sound of.

I pick up my phone and dial just as I see him in the distance, waiting under a tree and nervously checking his watch.

'Hello?' says Sean, answering, very uncoolly, after just one ring. He's wearing his best jacket and has Mitzy on a lead. I've got butterflies again. He looks . . . well . . . lovely.

'You might not like this . . .' I say, walking towards him.

He frowns a bit, worried about what I'm going to say.

'. . . But how do you feel about having a blob named after you?'

The end